\* \* \* \* \* \* \*

"Sam was murdered in Arizona."

"Murdered? I'm sorry. What happened?"

"He went to Arizona in search of some lost ancient treasure or something. He had gotten hold of an old map that told him where some Spaniards had hidden boxes of gold and Indian jewelry over four hundred years ago. He went to look for it. His body was found yesterday near a water hole at the base of Castle Dome in the Superstition Mountains."

"I'm sorry," I said, not knowing what else to say to her.

"There's more, Nick. According to police, it seems that Sam had a small piece of silver jewelry in his pocket that was shaped like a sun. It had little arrows coming out from the center of it. If what the police told me is correct, it could be a design used by an ancient Indian tribe that lived in that region six or seven hundred of years ago."

\* \* \* \* \* \* \*

Other titles by J.E. Terrall

| Western Short Stories | Western Novels |
|---|---|
| The Old West | Conflict in Elkhorn Valley |
| The Frontier | Lazy A Ranch |
| Untamed Land | (A Modern Western) |
| Tales From The Territory | The Story of Joshua Higgins |

| Romance Novels | Mystery/Suspense/Thriller |
|---|---|
| Balboa Rendezvous | I Can See Clearly |
| Sing for Me | The Return Home |
| Return to Me | The Inheritance |
| Forever Yours | |

Nick McCord Mysteries
Vol – 1 Murder at Gill's Point
Vol – 2 Death of a Flower
Vol – 3 A Dead Man's Treasure
Vol – 4 Blackjack, A Game to Die For
Vol – 5 Death on the Lakes
Vol – 6 Secrets Can Get You Killed

| Peter Blackstone Mysteries | Frank Tidsdale Mysteries |
|---|---|
| Murder in the Foothills | Death by Design |
| Murder on the Crystal Blue | Death by Assassination |
| Murder of My Love | |

# A DEAD MAN'S TREASURE
## Vol 3

## A Nick McCord Mystery
### by
### J.E. Terrall

ISBN: 978-0-9916232-2-8

Printed in the United States of America
First & Second Printing / 2009   www.lulu.com
Third Printing / 2014  www.creatspace.com

Book Layout /
Formatting:  J.E. Terrall
            Custer. South Dakota

# A DEAD MAN'S TREASURE

**A Nick McCord Mystery**

To my son, John

# CHAPTER ONE

I was lying awake in my bed with my hands behind my head as I stared up at the ceiling. In the quiet of my bedroom, I could hear the sound of the rain against my window, and the occasional sound of thunder off in the distance.

It was still dark outside, but I couldn't sleep. I'd been tossing and turning most of the night, but it was not the storm that kept me awake. Things had not been going very well at work. My mind was cluttered with thoughts of my job and my future.

I rolled over and sat up on the side of the bed. Looking across the room, I got out of bed and went to the window. Pushing the curtain aside, I leaned against the window frame and watched the rain as it fell into the puddles in the lighted parking lot below.

I had to wonder if Monica, my friend and lover, might have been right. She had suggested that I might consider looking for a new career in some other line of work.

I had talked with Monica on the phone just last evening. I was sure that she could understand my frustration with my job. We talked about everything from my taking a leave of absence, to quitting the police department all together. We must have talked for a couple of hours discussing the options available to me, but when all was said and done nothing had really been settled.

Being a policeman is certainly an honorable profession, but maybe it was time for me to look for something else. My job was no longer as satisfying as it had once been. I had almost found myself in the very same jail where I had put a number of criminals. Ever since I had been set up by a crooked cop to take the fall for the murder of a man, I felt something lacking in my job.

Although it had turned out okay and I had been able to prove my innocence, I was far more cautious about everything I did and said around other police officers. I was also more suspicious of others, civilians as well as officers. The trust that I once had in my fellow officers just didn't seem to be there any more. I seemed to have lost my edge. I was just doing the job that had to be done, and nothing more. It was as if I no longer had the ambition or the desire to continue.

My thoughts were suddenly interrupted by the harsh sound of my alarm clock going off. I walked over to the bedside table and shut it off. It was time to get up and get ready for work, but I was already up.

This morning was not like most mornings had been for me. I didn't want to go to work. I wanted to get away and have some time to think, to make some decisions and to put things in their proper perspective. I needed to re-evaluate my goals and decide what direction my life should take.

I thought about taking a short vacation as I had a lot of vacation time on the books. It seemed like it had been years since I had had a real vacation. With the caseload as heavy as it was at the precinct, I was sure that it would be hard to get Captain Joe Sinclair to let me have any time off.

I had just finished a case and turned in all the reports before leaving the office last night. I knew that as soon as I walked into the office this morning I would have another case handed to me to start working on. It had always been exciting for me to get a new case, but this morning the very idea of getting a new case was a depressing thought. The desire and the drive were gone.

I was about to go into the bathroom to take a shower when the phone started to ring. I sat down on the edge of the bed and picked up the receiver.

"Hello?"

"Nick. Oh, I'm so glad I caught you before you left for work."

"Monica?"

I knew it was her, but the urgency in her voice surprised me. We had just talked last evening and everything had been fine with her, but apparently everything was not fine now.

"Nick," she almost cried.

"What's the matter?"

"Do you remember Sam Kishler?"

"Yes, of course."

"He's - - - - he's dead."

"What?"

"Sam was murdered in Arizona."

"Murdered?"

I didn't know what to say. I didn't know Sam personally. I knew he was the head of the history department of the university where Monica worked, and that they were good friends. Sam had also been some help to me on an investigation a short time ago. Monica thought very highly of him and his ability, and I had found him to be a very pleasant sort of man when I talked to him over the phone.

"I'm sorry. What happened?"

"He went to Arizona in search of some lost ancient treasure or something. He had gotten hold of an old map that told him where some Spaniards had hidden boxes of gold and Indian jewelry over four hundred years ago. He went to look for it. His body was found yesterday near a water hole at the base of Castle Dome in the Superstition Mountains."

"I'm sorry," I said, not knowing what else to say to her.

"There's more, Nick. According to police, it seems that Sam had a small piece of silver jewelry in his pocket that was shaped like the sun. It had little arrows coming out from the center of it. If what the police told me is correct, it could be a design used by an ancient Indian tribe that lived in that region six or seven hundred of years ago."

"Do the police think that he might have found this, - ah - this treasure, or whatever he was looking for?"

"I don't know. About the only thing they were able to tell me was that he was murdered. Oh, they also said that he was not killed where his body was found. What does that mean?" she asked, her voice showing her distress.

"I'm not sure. It could mean almost anything. Did the police mention how he was killed?"

"No. They avoided answering those kinds of questions. Why would they do that?"

"That's hard to say. They may be keeping some of the details to themselves so if they catch someone and question them, only the killer would know the details. Do you know where he was searching for the treasure?"

"No, not exactly. He told me before he left that he was going to leave the original map in a safety deposit box in the bank. He said he made a special kind of map showing where he went, just in case."

"Just in case of what?"

"He didn't say. But Nick, I think he had some premonition that something might happen to him."

"Do you know where he left this "special map"?"

"No. It could be at his home or in his office, he never said."

"Do you have access to his office?"

"I could get in, I suppose. Do you want me to see if I can find it?"

"No. Don't go near his office. It could be dangerous."

"Nick?"

"Yeah, honey?"

"I know I'm asking a lot, but could you come here? I'm scared. Anyone who would kill someone like Dr. Kishler would stop at nothing to get what they want. Sam was a gentle man."

"Sure. Does anyone know that you know about the treasure map?" I asked.

"No. I don't think so."

"That's good. Keep it that way. Do the police have any leads?"

"I don't know. All I know is what I've told you. They weren't very interested in sharing very much information with me. I'll keep my eyes and ears open and see if I can find out anything else. Right now, you know as much as I do."

"You hang tight. I'll be there by early evening. I have a few things I'll need to clear up here first."

"Thanks, Nick. I love you."

"Honey, find out everything you can about what happened, what evidence the police have found so far, anything that might help. But whatever you do, don't show too much interest in what he was working on. I don't want you sticking your pretty little neck out," I said hoping that she would be careful.

"Okay. I'll keep my eyes and ears open."

The sound of her voice indicated to me that she was a little relieved that I would come so quickly.

"Great. Monica?"

"Yes?"

"Do I need to get a room at a motel?" I asked.

"No. I want you to stay with me. Do you mind?"

"No. Not at all. In fact, I was hoping that you would want me to stay with you."

"I do, Nick. Really, I do."

I found out where she lived and how to get there before I hung up the phone. Then I went to the bathroom to take a shower. My mind was full of thoughts of Monica. I could tell by the sound of her voice that she was worried, and maybe a little frightened. I certainly couldn't blame her for that.

As I thought of her, I began to think of us, the two of us. In doing so, I could not help but think about my situation. Maybe a few days with her, spending some time together, would help me to decide what I was going to do with my life. One thing that kept coming to mind was the thought that I wanted to find a way to keep her as a part of my life.

Gradually, my thoughts returned to what Monica had told me about the ancient treasure and the death of Doctor Kishler. A lot of questions came to mind. The first was, of course, who killed Sam? In order to answer that one, I would have to know who knew about the treasure map, besides Monica.

If Doctor Kishler had found the hidden treasure, someone would have had to trail him to it. They certainly would not want to kill him until he found it, unless, they simply killed him for the map.

I didn't know Doctor Kishler, other than to talk to him a couple of times on the phone. It would be my guess that being the outgoing type of man he seemed to be, he would probably have shared his information on such an important find with a close colleague. There was also the possibility that he shared it with more than one. The old adage that three can keep a secret if two are dead came to mind.

If someone with connections to the academic community was involved, that might mean there was a strong possibility that it was someone who had ties to the criminal elements as well. If my memory of history served me well, the real value of what would most likely be found in such a treasure would be its value as a rare artifact. There were those in the world who would give a great deal of money to have possession of rare artifacts, even if they could not show them in public. If that were the case, even the original map would be of great value as an artifact. I had no doubt that its market value would be a consideration to the murderers, and they could have killed him for the map alone.

The more I thought about it the more I realized that only an amateur, or someone very desperate for money, would steal rare artifacts just for the market value of any gold or gems that might be a part of it. I quickly realized that I needed to know more about the Spaniards and their conquests in that part of the country.

I also found myself very much interested in working on this case. It was not only an unusual case, which was the kind I liked, but it would be a challenging one. The fact that I would be working closely with Monica probably did a lot to help my enthusiasm.

I suddenly realized that I had become so engrossed in my thoughts that I had been standing in the shower much longer then I had planned and the water was getting cold. I got out and dried off.

While getting dressed, my thoughts turned to Captain Joe Sinclair and what he might say when I told him that I was going to take some time off. I was positive that he would not be willing to let me simply go to Madison for an unknown length of time without an argument.

It was at that moment that I realized that I might very well have to make my decision. I might have to decide what was really important to me, my job as a detective with the Milwaukee Police Department or my life with Monica. Given those choices, there was no question in my mind as to what my answer would be.

As soon as I was ready for work, I drove to the police building and went directly to my desk. Captain Sinclair was sitting at his desk in his office talking on the phone when I came in.

I sat down at my desk and looked at the stack of papers that had been put in my "In" basket. It was not going to be easy to tell Captain Sinclair that he was going to have to find someone else to handle my workload for a while, but I was prepared to do whatever was necessary so that I could leave for Madison by late afternoon.

"Morning, Nick."

I had been looking at the files in my "In" basket and had not seen Captain Sinclair approach my desk. I looked up and saw him standing in front of my desk. I noticed that he had a large envelope in his hand. There was no doubt in my mind what was in it.

"I have a case that I would like you to get started on right away," he said as he held out the envelope.

"I'm sorry, Joe, but I can't take on any cases right now. I have to go to Madison this afternoon. It seems there's been a murder of a university professor from Monica's department."

"What?" he said sharply.

I got the feeling that he didn't believe what I had just said to him.

"I have to go to Madison, and I don't know how long I will be gone," I said calmly, then waited for his reaction.

"Damn, Nick. I can't spare anyone right now. Let the local police handle it. You'll have to go see your girlfriend some other time. I need you here," he insisted.

I could see that he was not very happy with me, but on the other hand, I wasn't very happy here anymore, either. I knew I wasn't giving him any notice, but this was something I had to do. I had hoped that he would at least try to understand, but if he didn't, it didn't really matter. I had promised Monica I would come and I would keep my promise.

"I have to go. I don't know how long I will be gone. I have well over eight weeks of vacation time built up, and I haven't had a vacation for well over a year and a half. If you can't see your way to give me the time off to go, I'm going anyway."

I had thrown down the challenge. It was now up to him.

"I'm sorry, but I can't spare you right now," he said challenging what I'm sure he saw as a threat to his position of authority.

I looked at him, trying to decide if he meant what he said. I couldn't blame him for being upset with me. After all, I had put him in a bind, but no more of a bind than was usual around here. I also knew that there was never a good time to take a vacation with this job. We were always short handed. It was clear to me that he was not going to give me the time off I wanted.

"I guess you leave me no choice, Joe," I said as I stood up.

I reached inside my coat and took out the service issue pistol, the one that belonged to the department, and set it on the desk. Reaching into the inside pocket of my coat, I took my badge and ID out and laid it on the desk beside the gun.

"You're going to chase after that woman," he said not really believing that I was actually giving up my job for her.

"You're letting her lead you around by the nose," he added, the tone of his voice sounding demeaning.

His comments angered me a little. I wasn't being led around by the nose by anyone. I was not chasing after her, although I would be a damn fool if I didn't. I was simply going to the aid of a friend. I clinched my teeth and took in a deep breath in order to get control of my temper.

"I was hoping that it wouldn't come to this. With all the years we have known each other, you were the last one I expected to resort to cheap remarks like that. I'll send you my formal resignation in the mail," I said angrily. "You can consider me on vacation until you get my resignation."

I took a quick look at the desk to see if there was anything left that belonged to me. Since I've never been one to keep personal things at work, I didn't see anything that was mine. I turned and walked toward the elevator.

As I got into the elevator to go down to the garage, I looked back toward my desk. I saw Captain Sinclair standing there looking at me, the envelope still in his hand. I watched him disappear as the elevator door closed in front of me. I felt a little guilty walking off the job as I did, but this was something I had to do.

When I got to my car, I got in. I sat behind the wheel and looked through the windshield. I found myself taking one last look around. In a way, I was going to miss this place. After all, I had spent a good many years here.

I also knew that I had made my decision. Good or bad, I was going to have to live with it. Even though I felt guilty about leaving the way I did, deep down inside I think I knew it was the right thing for me to do.

I started my car and drove out of the police garage into the rain. To some people, the rain might have been considered a bad omen. To me, it was the sign of a fresh, clean start on a new life, and I was going to make the best of it.

As soon as I got home, I began to straighten up my apartment. I knew it was about a two-hour drive to Madison from Milwaukee, but I had this feeling that I would be gone for a very long time. After making the bed with fresh sheets, I went into the kitchen and began cleaning up. As I washed the dishes, the thought came to me that I might not be coming back here except to pick up my belongings.

The ringing of my phone suddenly disturbed my thoughts. I started toward the phone, but stopped at the door to the living room. I was reasonably sure that it would be Captain Sinclair, but I didn't want to talk to him right now. I hesitated, but decided to answer the phone just in case it was Monica.

"Hello."

"Nick, I want you to think about what you're doing?" Captain Sinclair said.

"Joe, I have. I've thought about it a lot over the past few weeks. I've made up my mind. I won't be coming back."

Suddenly, the phone went dead. I knew I had made him mad, but I had something I had to do. It was time for me to move on, to start a new career, whatever it might be.

I hung up the phone and went back to the kitchen to finish washing the dishes. Once I finished with them, I vacuumed the apartment and straightened up the newspapers and magazines. When I was satisfied that everything was in order, I went to the bedroom and began to pack for an extended stay with Monica.

As I rummaged through my dresser, I discovered that I still had the .32 caliber automatic that I had given my ex-wife when we first got married. After the divorce, she gave it back to me and told me she didn't want any guns around the house. My father had originally given it to my mother many years ago. I had kept it in the bottom of the dresser drawer and forgot about it until now.

Without thinking about it, I tossed the gun into my suitcase along with my underwear. I packed everything I would need and then looked around the place. Everything was in order. I couldn't think of anything I was leaving behind that I would need.

Satisfied that I was ready, I carried my luggage down the three flights of stairs and put it in the trunk of my car. I got in and backed out of the garage. As I drove out onto the street, I glanced back at the apartment. I had to wonder if I would ever come back here to live again.

It didn't take me long to get onto Interstate 94 and head west toward Madison. It was still raining and the wipers had all they could do to keep my windshield clear. I had thought about putting new wipers on, but never seemed to find the time to do it.

As I drove along the interstate, it was as if I were seeing a whole new world for the first time. I noticed that everything was green. The crops looked good, and the cows in the pastures had plenty to eat. It was funny, but these were the sorts of things that I never seemed to have had time to notice before.

As the miles rolled by, I began to think more clearly. It was as if getting out of the city and breathing some fresh country air was opening my mind to new thoughts and ideas. It was certainly a good opportunity to take a new and fresh look at myself, and what I wanted out of life. Maybe there was more to this trip to Madison for me than just another murder case. Maybe I needed this trip as much as Monica needed me, maybe more.

# CHAPTER TWO

I arrived in Madison about three-thirty in the afternoon. I knew I was a little early, but I wanted to get a look at the University of Wisconsin campus before I tried to find Monica's town house. At least that was the excuse I used to justify getting there so early. Actually, I was excited about seeing Monica again, but three-thirty in the afternoon was not "early evening" in my book. I didn't want to get to her place too early, although I don't know why. She seemed to want me to come as soon as possible.

I drove around the campus for a little while, but didn't find the History Department. It would have been easy for me to stop and ask someone, but I preferred to let Monica show me where it was located. I just drove around for a while to get the feel of the town more than anything.

When I was done driving around, I followed the directions that Monica had given me over the phone. I soon found myself in a rather expensive looking complex of town houses. They were very modern, and each one had its own garage. It was clear that my beat up old Dodge would stand out like a sore thumb in a place like this. I'd be lucky if I wasn't arrested for vagrancy as soon as I stopped the car.

It took me several minutes of driving through the narrow streets inside the complex to find Monica's town house. I noticed a visitor's parking sign and parked my car in front of it. As I got out of my car, I looked up at the fancy glass windows and semi-private balconies.

I had no idea how much a professor made, but from the looks of this place it was a lot more than I made. I had to chuckle at myself for that thought, because as of this morning I wasn't making anything. I was unemployed.

"Are you going to make me come down there and get you, or are you coming up here on your own?"

I looked up to see Monica standing on one of the balconies. She was the most beautiful sight I could ever hope to see. Her long blond hair gently waving in the breeze, the pleasant smile on her lovely face and the sound of her voice was all I needed to be reassured that she wanted me to be here.

I decided to leave my luggage in the car for now. I dashed across the parking lot and started up the stairs. When I reached the second story landing, she was at the top of the stairs waiting to greet me, and what a greeting it was. Monica threw her arms around my neck and planted a kiss on my mouth that I could feel clear down to my toes.

I wasted no time in grabbing hold of her. I wrapped my arms around her and held her tightly against me as we kissed. It felt good to have her in my arms again. I had not realized how much she meant to me until that very minute. She was the most important person in my life.

After several minutes of kissing and holding onto each other, we stepped back to look at each other. She took hold of my hands and smiled at me. I noticed that she was breathing hard, but then so was I.

"I'm so glad you could come," she finally said.

"I'm glad I could come, too."

"You want to get your things from the car?"

"I'll get them later. I just want to look at you."

Monica smiled. I could see in her beautiful cobalt blue eyes that she had missed me.

"Have you had dinner?" she asked.

"No. I thought we might go out and get something, if you haven't eaten."

"I have steaks and a salad all ready for us. I know you like steaks. All we have to do is grill the steaks," she said with a smile.

"Sounds good to me."

She let go of my hands as she turned around. As we started toward her town house, she slid her arm around behind me and I slipped my arm behind her as she led the way. Once inside, she let go of me and watched me as I looked around her place. I was sure she was wondering how I liked her home.

"This is very nice, very nice, indeed."

"I'm glad you like it."

I reached out and took her hand again. I pulled her toward me. As she stepped up in front of me, I let go of her hand and slid my hands onto her hips.

"God, I've missed you," I said as I pulled her up against me.

"I've missed you, too," she whispered as she wrapped her arms around my neck.

Monica tipped her head back as I leaned down to kiss her again. The feel of her shapely body and the warmth of her lips made me wonder why I had ever let this woman out of my sight, even for a minute. I must have been a fool.

After a long passionate kiss, she leaned back and looked up at me. I could tell by the look in her eyes that the reason for my being there had come back into her mind.

"I wish you were here just to see me," she said sadly.

"I would have come anyway. The death of Doctor Kishler just pushed me into it a little sooner."

"Are you sure?"

"Monica, I have something to tell you."

She didn't say anything. She simply looked at me and waited for me to speak. I wasn't sure how she would take it.

"I quit my job to come here. You needed me and I need you, so I came."

"You quit your job?"

"Yes."

She seemed surprised, but than why shouldn't she be. When we talked on the phone the other night we had talked about that as a possibility, but nothing had been settled.

"But why?"

"Sinclair wouldn't give me the time off to come. You needed me and I needed to get away from there. I wasn't sure what I should do, but I know enough to know that you are important to me."

"Am I really?" she said as she pressed her body against me and smiled up at me.

"Yes indeed."

"I love you," she whispered as she laid her head on my shoulder.

"I love you, too. You are the one stable thing in my life, the one thing that I am absolutely sure about. Everything else is kind of a jumbled up mess, right now. You offered me an opportunity to change my life for the better, and I took it," I said hoping that she would understand.

"I'm glad," she said as she squeezed me. "Will you look for a job here?"

"Maybe, but I don't think I will make any plans until after we see if we can find Sam's killer."

It felt good to just be holding her, but my mind would not let me forget why I had come. I wanted to find out what was going on and what she had found out. But for the moment, I just held her in my arms.

After a while, she let out a sigh. I was sure that she was ready to talk. I took hold of her by the shoulders and gently pushed her back so I could look at her lovely face.

"You ready to tell me what happened?"

"Yes, but come out to the kitchen," she said as she let go of me. "I'll finish fixing dinner while we talk."

"Okay. Is there anything I can do to help?"

"No. Just have a seat so we can talk. I know a little more than I did this morning."

I slipped my arm around her narrow waist and walked with her to the kitchen. I sat down on a barstool at the counter while she went around to the kitchen side of the counter.

"I found out early this morning that Sam Kishler had been murdered. That was when I called you. They found his body at a water hole near the base of Castle Dome in the Superstition Mountains. I think I told you that, too."

"Who are 'they'? Who found him?" I interrupted.

"Apparently, he was found by some people on an overnight jeep tour into the mountains. I guess they camp out at the water hole. Anyway, in the morning, one of them stumbled onto Sam's body partially hidden in some brush."

"Oh."

"When the State Police officers arrived at the scene, they found that Sam had been shot twice. He had been shot once in the back and once in the chest. They also said that there were so many tracks in the area from the people on the jeep tour that they could not find any clues as to how he got there.

"The only thing they seemed to be absolutely sure of was that Sam had not been killed at the water hole. He had been killed somewhere else, then taken there. So far, that's about all I have," she said sounding a little disappointed that she had not been able to find out more.

"You said something about a star-shaped piece of jewelry that was found on him. Do you know anything more about that?"

"I asked the Arizona State Police lab to fax me a photo of the piece of jewelry. They were reluctant to send it to me. But when I told them that I was an expert on old jewelry, they were a little more agreeable. It wasn't until I told them that I had worked with you on a case in Milwaukee that they finally decided to fax a photo of it to my office first thing in the morning. I had to promise to tell the investigating officer everything I could about it before he would agree to fax it to me," Monica explained.

"I didn't know that you were so well known by other police officers in other states. How is it that you are so well known in the police community?" she asked.

"I taught a class titled *"Gathering and Preserving Evidence at the Scene"* at the University of Wisconsin at Milwaukee a few years ago. A number of police officers from other states attended. I passed out a bunch of booklets as part of the class. The booklets had my name on them."

"Oh. I didn't know you were a published author and a professor, too," she said with a grin.

"I'm not, just well versed on the subject. Now, what about the map? Were you able to find out anything about it?" I asked.

"No. I was afraid to go to Sam's office and look around for it. There were just too many people hanging around his office," she said, again disappointed by her inability to get more information for me.

"What do you mean?"

"Sam's secretary was there most of the day. She was pretty upset by the news of Sam's death. Others from other departments were dropping in to ask if anything new had been found out about Sam, and to express their condolences to his secretary.

"Professor Garvey, one of Sam's closest friends, spent most of the day consoling Sam's secretary. Oh, Professor Campbell also dropped in, but he didn't stay very long. He was preoccupied with something else."

The tone of her voice and the look on her face when she mentioned Professor Campbell's name gave me cause to wonder about him. I couldn't be sure, but I got the impression that she either disliked him, or she didn't trust him. Maybe a little of both.

"Who's this Professor Campbell?"

"He's a young professor who thinks he's something special. He thinks he's God's gift to women, which I can assure you, he is not. He's always making passes at me. I don't like him very much."

"Is that why you don't like him?"

"Yes and no, well, not entirely. He has been trying to undermine Sam's authority in the department ever since Sam left for Arizona. He's a very ambitious man and I don't trust him. I don't think Sam trusted him, either."

"Why? There's nothing wrong with having ambition."

"No, there isn't. But he keeps trying to take credit for the things Sam has done. I even found him sitting in Sam's office, in Sam's chair. I think I caught him picturing himself in Sam's position as head of the department."

It was obvious by the expression on Monica's face that the thought of Campbell taking Sam's place as head of the department did not set too well with Monica.

"Was that before or after you found out about Sam's death?"

"After. It was this afternoon, just before I came home."

"Is it possible that he will get Sam's job?"

"He might," she replied after some thought. "If he does, I will quit. I will not work for him."

As I watched Monica fix dinner, I thought about what she had said. A promotion at his age to a department head at a large university would be a good size feather in his cap. It was not necessarily a motive for killing someone, but I have known people who have killed for a lot less.

"Now that Sam's gone, he's already talking about getting the university to finance a trip to the Superstition Mountains so that he can continue the search for the hidden treasure that Sam was looking for," she said as she set plates with steaks on them on the counter.

"I get the impression that you think he's after the treasure, if there is one. For the glory of finding it? To what end? To increase his prestige in the academic community?"

"Maybe. There's no doubt that it would increase his prestige, but I get the feeling that he's after the treasure more for himself than for the university," she said as she sat down next to me to eat.

"If the university finances him, he'll have to give what he finds to the university, won't he?" I asked.

"He's supposed to, but not if the university doesn't know what he found. He could hide some of the treasure, even all of the treasure, for himself and say he found nothing. Who would know the difference?"

"That's true enough. There wouldn't be anyone to prove otherwise. Do you think the university will finance him?"

"I seriously doubt it. Without the original map and proof that it is the real thing, they're not likely to put up the money."

"Sam had the original map, right?"

"Sure."

"Did the university finance his quest for the treasure?"

"No. I don't think so."

"Who did?"

"The word around campus is that he finances his own trips. Sam was not a poor professor. He had money in his own right. He didn't have to work at a professor's pay. In fact, he didn't have to work at all. He liked what he did. I think he would have done it without pay," she said.

"Do you know how he came into his money?"

"I believe he inherited it from his father. I think I remember being told that his father had been very wealthy. Sam was an only child and inherited everything."

I ate my salad and steak while we talked. There was much more to this than met the eye. I was sure of it.

Sam seemed to have been a fairly levelheaded sort of man, even if he had been a little eccentric. It sounded as if he had been a man not easily swayed or easily talked into things. The sort of a fellow who would have to have some proof, or some kind of assurance that what he was seeking really existed. I was convinced that he was not the sort of man that would waste his time on anything without something concrete to work with.

He also seemed to have been a rather cautious man. A man not prone to taking chances without careful consideration of all possible outcomes. If Sam had, in fact, made a "special map" for someone to follow after him and had placed the original map in a safety deposit box for safe keeping, he either had a copy of the original map with him or he had committed the original map to memory. Either way, there was a good chance that whoever killed him knew what he was looking for, and at least the area where it could be found. My question now was where was this "special map"?

It was clear to me that Sam would have put the "special map" in what he would consider to be a safe place. He would not put it in the safety deposit box with the original. He was too smart for that. If something happened to him, the courts would secure the safety deposit box until his will went through probate. That could take months.

Sam would have put his "special map" in a different hiding place. He would put it in a place where it could be found by someone he trusted. Someone who would follow up on it if something happened to him. At this point, I could think of only two possible places, his office and his home.

"What are you thinking," Monica asked.

I looked at her and realized that I had been staring off into space. I was also playing with my food and not eating.

"I was wondering what Sam might have done with this "special map" of his."

"I don't have any idea."

"Can we get into Sam's office after hours?"

"I doubt it. I don't have a key to his office."

"Can we get in the building without causing a big stir?"

"Sure. I often go to my office in the evening. The security guard wouldn't think a thing of it. My office is on the floor just below Sam's."

"Good. I think we'll take a trip to your office tonight."

I could tell by the look on Monica's face that she knew I had something on my mind. She was a smart woman. I would have been willing to bet that she could even figure out what I was thinking.

"Can we get up to Sam's office from yours without being seen?"

"I would think so. We could use the back stairs after they secure the building for the night. Are we going to look for the "special map"?" Monica asked.

"Yes."

"Where do you think it will be?"

"I don't have the slightest idea. We'll just have to look."

We finished eating in silence. I had a lot on my mind. The one thing I needed to learn was what made Sam tick. How he thought. If I could figure out how Sam's mind worked, I might be able to figure out what this "special map" was, and where he would have hidden it.

"Nick?"

"Yeah?"

"Even if we do find the map, won't we still be way behind the person who killed him? Wouldn't Sam's killer have had time to remove the treasure and get away before we could find it?"

"Yes, he would," I had to admit. "But if we do find the map, I'm sure it will help us find Sam's killer. I'm more interested in finding who killed him then I am in finding the treasure."

"Do you really think we can find his killer?"

"Honestly, Honey, I don't know. Right now, the special map is all we have to go on. We know where Sam's body was found. We know how he was killed. The Arizona State Police provided us with that information. What we don't know is who killed him, or where he was killed.

"The map might give us a clue as to where he was killed. That information could lead us to clues that might just point out who killed him. The best clues to a murder usually come from the scene of the crime, or from a witness.

I don't see that we will have any witnesses, at least not that we know of," I explained.

"I see. I guess we should go and try to find the map."

"Right."

I helped her clear the counter and stack the dishes in the sink as soon as we were finished with dinner. When we were finished cleaning up the kitchen, I retrieved my luggage from my car.

"You can put your suitcase in my bedroom, if you like," Monica said when I returned from my car.

"Are you sure you want me to stay here?"

"Oh, yes."

I smiled at her and then took my suitcase into her bedroom. I simply set it in the corner of her bedroom out of the way and then returned to the living room.

"You ready to go?" she asked.

"Yeah, but first I'd like a kiss."

Monica smiled and stepped up in front of me. As she reached out and put her hands on my shoulders, I reached out and put my hands on her narrow waist. I slowly drew her to me as I looked into her cobalt blue eyes. The smile faded from her face as I leaned down to kiss her. Our lips met in a warm, tender kiss.

Monica sort of melted against me. The feel of her beautiful body pressing against me erased everything from my mind, except her. It also made me wonder what a woman as beautiful as she was could see in me.

As our lips parted, she leaned back and looked up at me. A smile of contentment seemed to come over her face.

"I love you. I'm so glad you're here," she whispered. "I feel safe with you here."

That comment reminded me of why I had come here at this time. Monica was enough reason for me to be here. I had fallen in love with her the first time I met her. Only now did I really know how much I loved her. She was everything to me.

That thought caused me to worry. Once again, I felt as if I was dragging her into danger. I had no idea what I was getting into by taking on this case, but I was used to that. It had been part of my job as a policeman, and I had done it for years. She was not used to it.

That thought reminded me that I was no longer a cop. I had no authority to investigate this, or any other crime. Neither did she. I also knew that I had no choice. I had to find Sam's killer, if for no other reason than to make sure Monica would be safe.

"Are you ready to go?" I asked as I looked into her eyes.

"Yes," she replied softly.

She slipped her hands off my shoulders and took hold of my hand. Together, we walked down to the garage where she kept her car. When she opened the garage door, I couldn't help but smile at the sight of her little red sports car. It brought back some fond memories of when we first met.

"You drive," she suggested as she handed the keys to me.

We got in and I started the little car. Once out on the road, Monica directed me to the building that housed the history department of the university. When I pulled into the parking lot, she directed me to a parking spot. As I pulled in, I noticed the sign in front of the car. It read "Reserved for Dr. Barnhart".

"I'm impressed. You have your own parking space."

"Come on," she replied with a grin.

We got out and I looked up at the building. It was an impressive building. It was made of cut stone and brick and had pillars at the top of the long stairs in front. It looked like so many other university buildings across the country.

"This is it," she said as she took my hand and led me toward the building.

# CHAPTER THREE

Entering the State Historical Society building reminded me of entering a mausoleum. It was very quiet. The sounds of our shoes echoed in the halls as we walked across the marble floor toward the stairway to the basement.

"That's Sam's office in there," Monica said softly as she pointed toward a door.

I took a quick look at the door. It was an old wooden door with a frosted glass window in the upper half. On the window, in gold paint, was Sam's name and title. The brass lock concerned me a little, but I didn't think that it would be all that hard to open.

We turned and went through a heavy fire door into the stairwell, then down the stairs to the lower level. We passed through another door at the bottom of the stairs into a dimly lighted hall. It was obvious to me that this was not an area of the building frequented by visitors. Steam pipes, water lines and conduit ran along the ceiling and the walls, and were simply painted over. After going about halfway down the hall, Monica stopped in front of a door. Her name was on the door, "Professor M. Barnhart".

"This is it," she said as she reached into her purse for the key.

I waited for Monica to unlock and open the door then followed her into the room. I quickly noticed that the room was much more than an office. It was a large room that looked more like a storage room for old artifacts than an office.

There was a desk in one corner of the room that was cluttered with papers, and a large table with lots of over hanging lights that looked as if it was a place to examine and study different artifacts. I also noticed a large set of bookshelves that were filled with all kinds of reference books.

"Not much of an office, is it?" Monica commented.

"Oh, I don't know. It looks to me like a place where you could get a lot done."

"It is that," she agreed as she looked around.

"While we wait for the guard to close up the building for the night, do you have any material on the Superstition Mountains?" I asked.

"Sure. I did a little research into that this morning while I was waiting for you," she said as she walked over toward a small table in the corner.

"I suppose most of it is legend," I commented.

"Yes, but you have to remember that behind almost every legend there is some basis for fact. It's just that the facts often get lost in the legend. Sometimes to the point that what is fact becomes very difficult to find. Sometimes it can no longer be found.

"The Spaniards first explored Arizona in the 1540's. Francisco Vaquez de Coronado led a large expedition from Mexico into Arizona in search of the mythical Seven Cities of Cibola. There is some pretty strong evidence that he got as far north as about the Phoenix area. Some historians believe that he split up his expedition into two groups. One group of his expedition made it to the Grand Canyon, while the other group ranged as far north as Kansas. There is some evidence to support that belief.

"In the late 1590's, the land that includes Arizona and New Mexico was claimed for Spain by Juan de Onate. Missionaries were later established by Jesuit and Franciscan priests near Tucson and Phoenix," she explained.

"Wasn't there a mine somewhere in the Superstition Mountains that was supposed to be filled with gold?"

"Are you probably thinking of The Lost Dutchman Mine?"

"Yeah, that's it. Do you suppose that Sam was looking for it?"

"I wouldn't think so. There have been so many people looking for that mine, and so many maps supposedly showing its location, that I doubt Sam would be very interested in it. It would be almost impossible for anyone to prove that any given map was real. Sam would need something solid, something that would convince him that it was real before he would go off looking for it."

"Something like the piece of jewelry found in his pocket?"

"Possibly. Sam would be more interested in artifacts from the Spanish expeditions into the area than in a single lost mine. He had a lot of interest in the Spanish explorers. The legend of the lost mine is for those looking for riches," she explained.

"Don't you think that Sam might have gotten caught up in the wealth he could obtain by finding that mine, as well as the fame and glory?"

"No," she replied thoughtfully. "I guess it's possible, but I don't think so. I would hope that I knew him better than that. Sam never seemed to show much interest in wealth or what it could buy. He was more interested in the history, especially Spanish history as it pertained to the United States. He was more interested in learning about their expeditions into North America."

"Did the Spaniards get into the Superstition Mountains?"

"There is proof that they did, but what they found there has never been established with any degree of accuracy. Legend has it that they got into the mountains and found wealth beyond anyone's wildest dreams. But when they tried to take it out of the mountains, they were killed by the Indians that lived in and around the mountains at the time."

"What happened to this "wealth" that they found?"

"No one really knows. In fact, no one really knows if they actually found any wealth at all. Over the years, there have been a number of people who have gone into those mountains looking for it and found nothing. Some have gone into the mountains and never returned. Whether they were killed by the spirits that protected the treasures, as legend would have you believe, or they died from a lack of water has never been firmly established. It is very hard to separate fact from fiction when so little is known about what was really found."

As I thought about what she had said, I sat down at the table and began thumbing through one of the books that she had laid out for me. It was clear that the area around the Superstition Mountains was very desolate. From the maps of the area, it was also clear that there were very few roads in and out of the mountains.

As I looked at one of the maps, I began to think about where Sam's body had been found. I wondered what else was in that area. From the looks of the map I had in front of me, not much. It looked like nothing but wilderness, dry and deserted. With what little knowledge I had of the Arizona desert, I didn't really expect to find much.

"What do you think?" Monica asked, disturbing my thoughts.

"I don't know. Sam's body was found at a water hole at the base of Castle Dome, but he was not killed there. He could have been killed anywhere. Unless we find something that will give us a clue as to what he was doing down there and where he was doing it, I don't see much hope of finding his killer," I replied.

"I hope we find something," she commented.

"So do I. While we're waiting for the guard to close up the building, I think I'll read a few of these articles on the area where Sam was supposed to be. By the way, do you think that it's possible that he wasn't working in the Superstition Mountains at all? Maybe he just told you he was for some reason?"

"I don't think so. I'm sure he was pretty straightforward with me. Whenever he talked about his trip to Arizona, we were always alone. He never mentioned where he was going in front of anyone else that I know of. In fact, he insisted that I not tell anyone that he was even going to Arizona."

"Well, someone knew where he was going," I said.

I thought about Monica's last statement. That indicated to me that he trusted her. It also indicated that there were some people around here that he didn't trust.

"You said that he never mentioned where he was going in front of anyone else, does that include his secretary?"

"You know, I never once heard him mention his trip to her," she said after giving it some thought. "The more I think about it, whenever he talked to me about where he was going, we where here, in my office, not his."

The puzzled look on her face made me wonder why he would not confide in his own secretary. Did he know that she could not keep her mouth shut, or was there another reason?

"Sam's secretary - - -."

"Julie Gilbert."

"Yeah. How long had she been Sam's secretary?"

"I'm not sure, but she has been his secretary ever since I came here. I've been here almost six years."

"Then she's been with him for sometime. You would think he would trust her by now," I said thinking out loud. "I wonder why he wouldn't confide in her."

"It's possible that he knew that Professor Campbell and her were an item."

"You mean Sam's secretary has been seeing Professor Campbell?"

"Yes. I don't think it was common knowledge, though."

"How is it that you know?"

"It was quit by accident. I was working late one night and I saw them together in the parking lot. Campbell was standing along side Julie's car. I watched him lean inside and kiss her just before she drove off. Now that I think back on it, I find it a little strange. I didn't think much of it at the time."

"What did you think was strange?"

"Certainly not him kissing her. It was after he kissed her. He kissed her and as she started driving away, Campbell looked around as if he was afraid that someone might have seen them together."

"Are they both single?"

"Yes."

"Then why would he be concerned if anyone saw them together?"

"I don't know. Maybe he didn't want anyone knowing that he liked a lowly secretary."

"Maybe Professor Campbell didn't want anyone knowing that he had a spy in Sam's office, especially Sam."

"I guess that's possible," Monica agreed.

Professor Campbell had quickly moved to the head of my list of suspects, at least for now. He was ambitious all right, but was he a murderer? That was yet to be determined.

As far as Sam's secretary was concerned, my guess would be that she was just charmed by the smooth moves that Professor Campbell was putting on her. Sam must have known about Campbell's and Gilbert's relationship, otherwise why would he keep his trip a secret from her?

"It won't be much longer before the guard makes his rounds of the building and closes it for the night," Monica reminded me.

"Will he come into your office?"

"No, I don't think so. I'm usually gone by the time he makes his rounds so I don't know for sure. If we shut off all the lights except the one over the work table, he should just check the door and go on."

I walked across the room and opened the door. After I looked out into the hall to see if anyone was there, I reached over and shut off the ceiling lights. As I closed the door, I noticed that Monica had shut her desk light off. I turned the knob that locked the door, and then went across the room to Monica.

"Does the guard have a key to your office?"

"I'm sure he does. He has a key to all the offices."

"Okay. Maybe we should hide behind those shelves until we're sure he has made his rounds, just in case he looks in," I suggested.

Monica nodded in agreement. We went around behind the shelves and sat down on the floor. As I leaned back against the shelves, Monica leaned up against me. I put my arm around her and held her close to me.

"You sure have a funny way of getting a girl to cuddle up to you," she whispered.

"Hey, it works," I whispered.

Monica looked up at me. The smile on her face slowly faded as I leaned closer to her. She closed her eyes as our lips touched in a soft gentle kiss. Our kiss slowly grew more passionate as the seconds ticked by.

Our moment of passion was suddenly disturbed by the sound of someone rattling the door. We both looked toward the door, wondering if the guard was going to open it and check the office, or just go on down the hall. We waited. I could hear the guard slip a key into the lock. He opened the door, stuck his head in and looked around inside, and then closed the door again. I could hear him locking the door. We could see his shadow on the window of the door as he turned and moved way. We could hear his footsteps as he went on down the hall.

"How long do we wait?" Monica asked in a whisper.

"It will most likely take him an hour to make sure the building is secure. We'll wait a little longer than that."

Monica cuddled up against me and relaxed. I wrapped my arm around her shoulders and leaned back against the bookshelves again. While we waited, I let my mind wander. I had a lot to think about.

It was strange, but at this moment I didn't feel like I was among the unemployed. I guess I didn't really have time to think about a job. It was probably because I was working on a case, something that I normally would be doing. The fact that I would still be getting a paycheck until my vacation time ran out didn't hurt any, either.

I spent the quiet time thinking and mulling over in my mind the area where Sam's body was found. It was clear why they wanted his body found. It was to prevent a full scale search of the mountains for him. What was not clear was why his body had been taken to the water hole where it was sure to be found, unless whoever killed him wanted him found very quickly. That might also make sense if the killer wanted to direct any investigation away from where he was really killed.

I listened for any sounds, but I heard nothing. The building was quiet. No more doors opening and closing, no more footsteps in the hall. It was time, time to check out Sam's office.

"Honey, it's time to go," I whispered.

Monica sat up and looked at me. I smiled at her and then stood up. After helping her to her feet, I took her hand and lead her to the door. I slowly and quietly unlocked the door. Taking the doorknob in my hand, I turned it. Once the latch was loose, I slowly opened the door and looked out into the hall.

"Looks clear," I whispered. "Which is the best way to Sam's office?"

"Down the hall to the left. We'll take the back stairway up to his office," she whispered.

"Lock the door," I said before I led the way out into the hall.

After stepping out into the hall, I waited while she locked the door behind us. I then started down the hall with Monica close behind. We moved along as quietly as possible, listening for any sound that might give us notice that someone was nearby.

Once we reached the top of the stairs, I slowly pushed open the door into the hall. I quickly checked out the hall, it was empty. I started to move out into the hall, but stopped at the sound of footsteps.

"Someone's coming," I whispered as I quickly ducked back into the stairwell.

We leaned back against the wall and hoped that whoever was out there did not want to use the staircase. We held our breath as the guard walked by the stairwell door and on down the hall.

I looked at Monica and let out a sigh of relief. I could see that she had been a little worried, too.

We didn't move for several minutes, giving the guard time to get where he was going. Once I was fairly certain that he was gone, I again slowly pushed the door open and peered out into the hall. The hall was clear.

"I want you to wait here until I get the door open," I whispered.

"The second door down. The one that says 'Private' on it is the door directly into Sam's office. The door with his name on it is the door to his outer office," Monica informed me.

I was glad to hear that. It would put me closer to the stairwell if the guard should return before I could get the door open. I would also have a better chance of getting away if I had to make a run for it.

I nodded that I understood, then stepped out into the hall. The first door I passed had a sign on it that read "Women", the second one read "Private". I looked up and down the hall as I reached into my pocket. I pulled out a small leather folder. After taking out the instruments that I needed, I quickly and quietly picked the lock and opened the door.

After another quick look up and down the halls, I motioned Monica to join me. I kept an eye out as she came down the hall toward me.

When she was about half way, I heard the sound of footsteps. Someone was coming down the hall around the corner. I motioned for Monica to hurry. As she hurried past me, I stepped inside Sam's office and pulled the door closed. I was careful not to allow the door to latch. I was afraid that if the latch made any sound at all, the guard would be checking out all the doors in the hall.

We leaned back against the wall and stood there holding our breath. We looked at each other as we waited for the sound of the footsteps to fade away on down the hall.

"That was close," Monica whispered.

"It sure was. Come on, we have work to do."

"You want me to start in the outer office?"

"No. I think we should work together. I'm not sure what we're looking for."

"Neither am I."

I looked around the room. I didn't know what I was looking for, but I was hoping that something would grab my attention. Most of the walls of the room were covered with bookshelves. One wall had several plaques and a number of small photographs.

There was also a large painting on the wall that did grab my attention. It had a light shining on it that helped to light up the room a little. I walked over in front of the painting and stood looking at it. It was clear to me that it was a painting of some mountains, probably in the southwest. It looked very familiar to me, but I couldn't place it.

"That's a painting of the Superstition Mountains," Monica whispered as she moved up next to me.

"It looks familiar. I'm sure I've seen this before."

"You've probably seen a number of pictures of those mountains from about the same angle. It's a popular view. That's the way they look from the highway between Globe

41

and Apache Junction. I think most of the postcards from that area have that same view of the mountains on them."

"Is that an original painting?"

"Yes. Sam did that painting a few years ago."

"You mean he painted it, himself?"

"Yes. He's pretty good, don't you think?"

"Yes. Yes, he was."

The fact that he had painted the picture himself got me to thinking. That picture might very well hold the key to where Sam had been.

I took a few minutes to look at the small photos on the wall. Several of them were of him and several other people standing in what looked like a desert. In the background of one of the photos was part of the Superstition Mountains. That photo confirmed my suspicions that he knew his way around those mountains, or at least he had been there more than once.

I also discovered that there were a number of black and white photos that looked like they were of the same area. My first thought was why would anyone take pictures of jagged crags and narrow trails along rocky cliffs with no one in the pictures. It was as if he had taken pictures of an unmarked trail.

Then it came to me. Sam had made a photo map of where he had been and hung it on his wall where everyone could see it. The phase "Hidden in plan sight" came to mind. My guess was that if we found each one of those places, we could find our way. But our way to what? What had Sam found that made him go to all the trouble of making a photomap?

"Monica, do you know when these pictures were taken?"

"I don't know for sure. He put them up just after he took his vacation last summer.

"Were these others taken at the same time?" I asked as I pointed to another set of pictures.

"No. They were taken two years ago."

"Who are these people in the pictures?"

"Well, this one is Professor Garvey," she said as she pointed to a man that was obviously overweight, balding, and somewhat shorter then the others in the group.

"And this is Professor Campbell."

Campbell looked like the typical great white hunter. He was wearing sharply pressed khaki colored pants and jacket, and matching wide brimmed hat. I couldn't help but think that he looked like an amateur on his first trip into the wild.

"Who is this?" I asked as I pointed to a third man in one of the pictures.

"I believe that was Professor Jacob Martin. I've never met him. He was a very close friend of Sam's. I believe he was from the University of Minnesota."

"You keep saying "was"?"

"That picture was taken very close to the beginning of a trip into the mountains. He died on that trip shortly after they started out. The story is that he was in a cave and part of the roof collapsed on him."

"Did Sam ever tell you what he thought happened?"

"No, not really. He just said that Martin would never have let himself get into a position where that would happen. He was too experienced a geologist for that."

"I take it Sam didn't believe that Martin's death was an accident?"

"I don't think he did, but he could never prove it. Sam was not the type to go around making accusations without some kind of proof. He kept things like that pretty much to himself," Monica said.

"Who is this man? He looks like he might be an Indian."

"That would have to be Juan Vasquez. He was their guide. I understand that he has lived around there all his life."

"Let's see what else we can find," I suggested. "I'd like to have copies of each of these pictures," I said as I pointed out the ones with no one in them.

"I can copy them in the outer office on the copy machine while you look around," Monica suggested. "They might not be as detailed, but they should be pretty clear since they are black and white," she said.

"Good idea. If you hear anyone coming, get back in here. And be sure to hang the pictures back on the wall where you got them."

"I will," she replied.

While Monica took down each of the pictures to make copies, I started looking through Sam's desk. I found it interesting that it was not locked.

It could be a long night. There was a lot to search. It was made even more difficult by the fact that I had no idea what I was looking for. Something in the back of my mind told me that I was not likely to find a map here. At least not a map like I was used to seeing. The pictures were the closest things we had to a map. But they would be of little value since we had no idea where to start from and what order to put them in. Unless the pictures were numbered, or there was some way for me to know what order they were taken in, there was little hope that they would be of much help.

After Monica finished copying the photos, she helped me painstakingly go through the stacks of files and papers in Sam's Office. We even searched the outer office on the outside chance that we might find a clue there. We turned up nothing that we felt would help us.

After several hours of searching, all we found that would give us any kind of a clue as to where Sam might have gone were the black and white pictures on the wall in his office. Even those were of little value unless we could figure out how to use them.

"I think we've done all we can here," I told Monica. "Let's get out of here."

"Okay," she replied with a big sigh of disappointment.

Monica walked to the private entrance to Sam's office and waited for me. I took one last look around to make sure that we had left no sign that we had been there. As soon as I was satisfied that everything was in order, I joined Monica at the door.

"Ready?"

"Yes," she replied with a whisper.

"How do we get out of here?"

"I hadn't thought about that," Monica said. "All the outside doors will be locked. If we don't get let out by the guard, we'll set off an alarm."

"We don't want to set off any alarms. That will certainly make us look like we were doing something shady. If we just go to the guard desk and ask to be let out, we won't draw near as much attention to ourselves."

"I guess we have to go by the guard desk," Monica agreed. "The only question I have is how will we explain being here?"

"We'll just tell the guard that we got so wrapped up in our research that we lost all track of time."

"You think it will work?"

"Never know until you try." I replied with a grin.

"Okay. Let's go."

I took a moment to listen for any sounds that would indicate someone was in the hall, but I heard nothing. I opened the door very carefully and peered out. There was no one around. I motioned for Monica. As soon as she stepped out into the hall, I closed and locked the door again.

I took Monica by the arm and we started down the hall as if we were supposed to be there. We made no attempt to be quiet. As we turned the corner, I could see the guard's desk near the front door.

"I don't know if I really believe that we have been visited by beings from outer space or not," I said as we came around the corner.

"But there is a lot of evidence - - -."

Monica was interrupted by the voice of the security guard as he stood up.

"What are you doing in here?   Oh, I'm sorry, Doctor Barnhart," the guard said as he suddenly realized who was coming toward him.

"Oh, hi, Jerry."

"What are you doing here so late?" he asked as he looked from her to me.

"I was doing a little research to prove a point to my friend. Oh, I'm sorry. Nick, this is Jerry Miller, one of our security guards. Jerry, this is Detective Nick McCord of the Milwaukee Police Department."

"Nice to meet you, Jerry."

"Nice to meet you, too, sir."

"Would you be so kind as to let us out?  We got so wrapped up in what we were doing that we sort of lost track of time," Monica explained.

"Sure," Jerry said as he reached for his keys.

We followed the guard to the door, then waited while he unlocked the door and let us out.  Once outside we walked down the steps and around the corner to Monica's car.

"Nice job, introducing me as a detective from Milwaukee," I said with a grin.

"Well, I didn't lie.  You are still a detective from Milwaukee, at least until your vacation time runs out," she said with a grin as she squeezed my arm.

We got into her car and headed back to her place. It was pretty late. Actually, it was pretty early in the morning by the time I drove the car into the garage.

As we walked to Monica's town house, she held onto my arm. I was feeling pretty tired. It had been a long day for me, and I was sure it had been a long day for Monica.

We no more then stepped into her town house then Monica yawned. I couldn't help myself, I yawned, too.

"I think we better get some sleep. We have a lot to do tomorrow," Monica suggested.

"You're right about that," I agreed as I dropped the envelope with the copies of the photos on the end table.

"Do you know where Sam lived?" I asked Monica as I followed her into the bedroom.

"Yes. Do you think we should go there tomorrow?" she asked as she pulled her top up over her head and tossed it over a chair.

"Did he live alone?" I asked as I took off my shirt.

"I think so. He has an apartment on the other side of Lake Mendota."

I found it difficult to take my eyes off her as she finished undressing. She smiled at me as she turned and went into the bathroom. When she returned I watched her come toward me.

"You are the most beautiful creature I have ever seen," I said as she stepped up in front of me.

"Thank you," she replied with a smile as she reached out and put her hands on my shoulders.

I reached out and put my hands on her narrow waist and drew her close to me. She slid her hands around behind my neck and tipped her head back. I leaned down and kissed her.

The feel of her warm lips against mine, and the feel of her warm body pressing against me was all it took for her to have my complete and undivided attention.

Monica leaned back and looked up at me. Her eyes told me that she loved me, but her body told me that she wanted me.

"I've been waiting all day for this moment," she whispered breathlessly. "Take me to bed."

I didn't say a word. I simply scooped her up in my arms and laid her down on the bed. As I lay down beside her, she wrapped me in her arms and drew me down over her. This was our time to love, and make love.

# CHAPTER FOUR

The sun had been up for some time when I woke. As I lay beside Monica, I could feel the warmth of her naked body against me. She was curled up next to me with her head on my shoulder and her hand resting on my chest. I could smell the pleasant fragrance of her blond hair and feel its softness against my skin.

I wanted to touch her, to feel the smoothness of her skin under my hand, but I didn't want to wake her. I liked having her lying against me. It gave me a contented feeling that consumed me and made me wish that it would never end.

Staring up at the ceiling with my mind wandering, I wondered if it could be like this for us forever. The thought of marriage crossed my mind, but I was not sure about it. I loved her more than anything in the world, but I had had one marriage that turned out badly. I knew that to compare what we had with my former marriage was not right. There was so much difference between Monica and Sharon, but still, once burned, twice shy as the saying goes.

"What are you thinking about?" Monica asked in a whisper.

The soft, concerned sound of her voice interrupted my thoughts. It would have been a perfect time for me to ask her to marry me, but I just couldn't bring myself to say the words.

"Nothing special," I replied.

"Are you ready to get up?"

"Sure."

"Good, because I'm starving. Give me a few minutes, then the bathroom's yours," she said.

Monica raised herself up, then rolled over on top of me. I wrapped my arms around her as I drew her to me. The feel of her firm breasts pressing against my chest and her naked body stretched out over me, sent a new wave of desire through me. I would have preferred to stay right there for the rest of the day, but I knew that was impractical. We had too much to do. Besides, she had already made it known that she was hungry. I had to admit that I was hungry, too.

After a long passionate kiss, she rolled off me. She sat up on the edge of the bed and looked back over her shoulder at me. She smiled.

"I'll be out in a few minutes, then you can have it," she said as she stood up and went into the bathroom.

I laid in bed with my hands behind my head. I keep thinking about her, but then why wouldn't I? She was the most beautiful and intelligent woman I had ever met, and she was the best thing to happen to me in years. I had to wonder what it was that she could see in me, a plain ordinary man. This was one very special lady, and I would be a fool to let her get away.

As I lay there waiting for Monica to come out of the bathroom, my thoughts came around to what had happened yesterday. I couldn't help but remember what we had done together, including the searching of Sam's office and what we had found there. I suddenly found myself thinking about Sam and who might have killed him.

We had found nothing in his office that we thought would help us, except for the photos. Our plan for today was to search his apartment in the hope of finding something, anything that would put us on the path to finding the person or persons who killed him. I had serious doubts that we would find anything important in Sam's apartment, but we had to at least look.

My thoughts were disturbed by Monica as she came out of the bathroom. I looked up at her as she smiled down at me. She was wearing that same robe that I liked to see her in, the one that accented the smooth lines of her lovely figure and showed just a bit of cleavage.

"Time to get up. What would you like for breakfast?" she asked as she smiled down at me.

"You?" I asked playfully as I reached out and grabbed the bottom of her robe.

"You already have me. How about some eggs and toast?"

"Is that all you're offering?"

"That's all I'm offering this morning. I might offer something more interesting later on," she said with a sexy smile.

"I can hardly wait for "later on"," I said as I let go of her robe.

"Come on. We have things to do," she said with a grin.

"Okay, slave driver."

She threw me a kiss, then turned to leave. I watched her as she walked out of the bedroom. She was right and I knew it. We had a lot to do if we were going to find out what Sam was looking for in the Arizona desert, and who had killed him.

I got up, went into the bathroom and took a quick shower then shaved. When I was finished, I returned to the bedroom and found the bed had been made. I also noticed that she had set my suitcase on the foot of the bed. I opened it up and began rummaging around in it.

As I picked out what I was going to wear, I stumbled onto the small .25 caliber pistol that I had tossed in my suitcase when I packed. My first thought was to give it to Monica, but I was not sure if she would want it. I knew she wasn't afraid of guns, but I didn't know if she knew how to use one.

The thought crossed my mind that I should take her somewhere where I could teach her how to use it safely. I had no idea what we might be getting into. If she knew how to handle a gun, I might feel a little better about her getting so deeply involved. I certainly hoped that she would never need it, but it was best to be safe.

Without giving it any further thought, I covered it up again before closing my suitcase. I then dressed and went out to the kitchen where I found Monica standing in front of the stove.

"You look very domestic this morning," I said as I stepped up behind her.

I slipped my arms around her narrow waist as I leaned over her shoulder to see what she was cooking. I could feel her lean back against me as she put the eggs on the plates.

"I certainly could be for the right person."

I wasn't sure how to take her comment. I wanted to ask her if I could be that person, but decided to drop the subject for now. I wasn't sure I was ready to hear her answer. Instead, I kissed her lightly on the neck and let go of her.

"What can I do?"

"You can sit down."

I sat down at the small table and watched her as she turned around. She had two plates in her hands. Each plate contained a couple of eggs, a couple of slices of toast and a sausage patty. She set one plate in front of me, then set the other plate across the table. After pouring coffee for us, she sat down across from me.

"What do you hope to find at Sam's apartment?" she asked as we started eating.

"I'm still hoping to find the map. I doubt that it will be there, but I have to look. Other than that, I have no idea," I admitted.

We ate our breakfast and didn't say very much for a while. I had finished my eggs and sausage when a thought suddenly crossed my mind.

"Didn't you tell me yesterday that the Arizona State Police was going to send a fax to your office this morning?"

"Oh, yes. I forgot all about it."

"I think we should stop by your office and get it before someone else finds it."

"Good idea."

After we finished our breakfast, Monica got dressed. We hurried back to the State Historical Society building. As soon as Monica unlocked and opened the door to her office, she rushed across the room to her fax machine. There in the tray was a fax. As she picked it up and looked at it, I looked at it over her shoulder.

"This is unbelievable," she said excitedly as we looked at the fax.

"What's unbelievable?"

The sound of a male voice startled both of us. As we turned around, I noticed that Monica hid the fax behind her back.

Standing just inside the door was a well-dressed man. He was sort of a handsome fellow with a disarming smile. He was wearing a suit that couldn't be purchased at any J.C. Penney's I've ever been in, and a silk shirt and tie. There was something about him that told me that I was not going to like this guy. He looked just a little too smooth for me.

"Excuse me. Who's your friend, Monica?" he asked, as he looked me over.

"Oh, this is Detective Nicholas McCord from the Milwaukee Police Department."

I noticed the man's expression changed slightly, and the grin on his face faded with her mention of the word "detective". I got the distinct impression that he didn't like the idea that I was a policeman. I think it made him just a little bit nervous.

"Detective McCord, this is Professor William Campbell."

I caught the way she introduced me. Again, her emphasis was on the detective part of her introduction.

"How do you do?"

"I'm fine. What brings you to Madison, Detective McCord?"

"I've been asked to look into the death of Professor Samuel Kishler," I said as if I had all the authority in the world to do just that.

"Oh, really?"

"Really," I confirmed.

I thought I saw a little squinting in his eyes, a sign to me that he was not thrilled that I was there. I'm sure the idea of an investigator right there in his building, especially an investigator from the outside, didn't set too well with him. I got the impression it just might have brought the investigation a little too close to home to suit him.

"Yes," Monica added.

"At whose request, may I ask?"

His question was simple enough, but I got the impression that he was really asking if I was there to investigate him. I'm sure he also wanted to know if I was there in an official capacity.

"I'm sorry, but I not allowed to divulge that information at this time. I'm sure you can understand."

"Oh, Yes. Yes, of course," he replied, a little surprised by my answer.

I had to almost laugh at the confused look on his face. I'm sure he had expected me to answer his question. I got the feeling that he was surprised that I was smart enough not to answer him without thinking about it first.

"Ah. Oh, by the way, what was so unbelievable?" he asked.

I'm sure he posed the question in an effort to try to regain control of the situation. If that was the case, he was in for a surprise.

"It was nothing that would interest you," Monica said with a polite smile.

"Everything interests me," he replied with a forced grin.

"It was actually for me," I said flatly.

I noticed the change in his expression. The stupid grin on his face disappeared. The way he looked at me caused me to wonder if he might want to challenge my authority. His eyes narrowed slightly again as he looked at me, but I didn't give. I got this gut feeling that Professor Campbell and I were going to have a serious confrontation, sooner or later. It wouldn't be now and it might not even be tomorrow, but we were going to meet head to head before this was all over.

Professor Campbell looked over at Monica, then back at me. It was clear that he wasn't sure what his next move should be. He must have decided that he would retreat for now. We had made it clear that we were not going to share what we had with him.

He turned and started for the door. When he reached the door, he stopped and turned back toward us. He looked at me and acted like he wanted to say something, but then looked over at Monica.

"You still work for the university, don't you?" his voice once again in full control.

"Yes, of course."

"Then I want to see you in my office in five minutes," he said in a demanding tone.

He then turned back around and walked out the door without waiting for a response. I looked at Monica and she looked at me. I wondered what was going on. From the look on Monica's face, she was just as confused and concerned as I was.

"I'll be right back," she said as she handed me the fax.

"What's going on?"

"He thinks he's the boss now that Sam's gone."

"Is he?"

"He might be, but I'm not one of his slaves. Shortly after he was hired, I told Sam that I would never work for him, and I won't."

I noticed a strong tone of determination in Monica's voice. I doubted that she was one to let this guy treat her like she was one of his servants. There was no doubt in my mind that she was a strong willed woman, and that she was not about to be pushed around by the likes of him.

"You want me to wait here or come with you?"

"Wait here, please."

"Okay. If you need me, let me know."

"I do need you, but I can handle this," she replied with a smile.

She leaned toward me and kissed me lightly on the lips. I gave her a wink in the hope of providing her with at least a small measure of encouragement and a little moral support. She was one smart lady. I was sure that she would do whatever she thought was right. Campbell may be a smooth character, maybe even clever, but I doubted that he would be able to intimidate Monica.

While I waited for her to return, I looked at the fax. It was a copy of a photograph of a very interesting piece of jewelry. Although it didn't mean very much to me, I was sure that it must have meant a great deal to Monica. She seemed very impressed when she first saw it.

I folded the fax up and put it in my pocket. I then began to look at some of the books that she had stacked on the worktable. Although I flipped through some of them, my mind was on Monica and what was going on in Campbell's office. I didn't like the idea of her being alone with him. I didn't trust him, but on the other hand I had confidence in Monica and her judgment.

I didn't have long to wait to find out what had happened. Suddenly, the door flew open with a crash and Monica stormed into the room. It was clear that she was mad as hell.

"That arrogant, conceded, little pompous ass had the nerve to tell me to get rid of you. You know what he said?" she asked more to make a point than to get an answer.

"No."

"He told me that we didn't need some hotshot cop nosing around here and stirring up trouble. I found it interesting that he knows who you are. He's read about you in the Milwaukee paper."

"Do you think we made him a little nervous?"

"I think we did," she replied with a grin as she realized what she had said. "He's afraid of something. He's so afraid that he not only wants you out of here, but he wants me out of here, too."

"You?"

"When I wouldn't tell him what was on the fax, he got real hot under the collar. The veins in his neck stood out and his face got red. He must have asked me three or four times what was on the fax and where it had come from. When he finally got the message through his thick skull that I wasn't going to tell him, he told me that he had been appointed as the new interim department head. That's when he told me if I wasn't going to cooperate with him and show him what was on the fax, I could pack my things and get out."

"Can he do that?"

"No. Not without a hearing for cause."

"What did you tell him?"

"I told him that he was an arrogant, conceited, pompous ass, and that he would never be half the man that Sam was. I also told him that there was no way in hell that I would work for the likes of him," she said, her voice showing her agitation.

"So, I guess you're out of a job, too?"

"Yes, I guess I am," she said with a grin.

"Now what?"

"Will you help me pack up what's mine so we can get out of here?"

"Sure."

I was more than willing to help her pack, but that was not what was bothering me. Because of me, she was out of a job. I had a little money saved up and could get by for some time without a job, but I was worried about her. I had no idea what her financial situation might be.

Before I knew what was happening, she handed me a box. I looked at the box, then at her. She must have seen the dumb look on my face.

"Every book on that shelf right over there is mine," she said pointing to a shelf behind me. "If you'll pack them in these boxes, I'll pack up my other things."

"Okay."

I took the box, then watched her as she went to her desk. She seemed to be taking this very well, but I was still worried about her. This had been her whole life and now it was over. I figured that it might take a while before all of this soaked in. She would not be coming back here to work again. Her job here was over. All I knew for sure was that I needed to be here for her when she needed me.

I went to the shelves that she had pointed out and began taking the books off them. I neatly packed them in the boxes. I quickly noticed that they were reference books on all sorts of subjects ranging from jewelry, to pottery, to paintings. There were books about lost civilizations, ghost towns, legends and mysteries of the unknown. I didn't know there were so many reference books on those subjects. You name it, it was there. By the time I was finished packing the books, I had four boxes of them.

As I was putting the last book in the last box, I looked over at Monica. She was sitting on the chair in front of her desk staring at a picture. I was sure that I could see a tear in the corner of her eye. I stood up and walked over to her.

Standing behind her, I put my hands on her shoulders and looked over her head. The picture she was looking at was of Sam and her holding the painting of the Superstition Mountains that now hung in his office.

"He was a good friend," she sobbed. "I'm going to miss him."

I didn't know what to say. Times like this always left me feeling kind of useless. I simply massaged her shoulders in the hope that I was bringing some small measure of comfort to her.

Monica started to put the picture in the box she was packing when something caught my eye. I wasn't even sure what it was, but I needed to see that picture again.

"Wait. Let me see that, please."

Monica seemed surprised at my request, but took the picture back out of the box. She looked at it again while she held it so I could see it.

"Look at where he's pointing."

"I don't see anything. He's just pointing at the picture," she said, not sure what I was getting at.

"Are you sure? Is it possible that he's pointing at the location where the photo map starts?"

I wasn't sure that I was even close to being on the right track here, but I had to look at all the possibilities no matter how obscure they might seem. And this seemed very obscure.

"I can't say for sure," Monica said with a tone of frustration and interest in what I was thinking.

"Let's leave it for now. We can take a closer look at it later," I suggested.

Monica put the picture back in the box. I took the box and set it with the others, then looked around.

"Do you have everything that belongs to you?" I asked.

She looked around her desk, then at the bookshelves.

"I think so. Oh, wait."

She stood up and walked over to the fax machine. She pressed several buttons, then the machine began to print out a sheet of paper.

"What's that?"

"It's a ledger. It gives a list of all the faxes that have come over this machine since the last ledger was printed, and where they came from. It should give us the fax number of the Arizona State Police lab."

"Good thinking. Can you clear that information out so no one else can get it?"

"Sure. Once I've printed the ledger, it's gone from the machine."

"Great. Now Campbell won't be able to find out where that last fax came from."

Once the fax machine finished printing, Monica handed the ledger to me. I folded it and put it in my pocket with the other fax. One more look around and we were ready to leave.

I noticed a two-wheel handcart in the corner. I stacked the boxes of books on the cart along with the box Monica had packed. I rolled the cart to the door and waited for Monica to take one last look around.

"You got everything?"

"Yes. Let's get out of here."

Monica seemed to be in a hurry to leave. I guess I couldn't blame her. She opened the door and I wheeled the cart out into the hall. We took the elevator to the main floor and stopped at Sam's office. I noticed Campbell standing inside the outer office, and Julie was sitting at her desk. Campbell seemed very much interested in what was on the cart, but Julie just looked lost.

I waited as Monica stepped into the outer office. She passed right by Campbell without so much as looking at him. She dropped the keys on Julie's desk, then turned on her heels and walked out. She didn't say a word to either one of them.

Monica took me by the arm and we left the building. After loading the boxes in the car, I turned the cart over to one of the security guards. I thanked him for taking it back for me, then got into the car.

We left the parking lot and drove back to Monica's town house. Monica did not say a word. She sat quietly and looked out the windshield. I was a little worried about her. I was sure that this morning was hard for her.

When we arrived at Monica's town house, we carried the boxes of books into the house. We stacked them just inside the door. When we were finished, I sat down on the sofa and motioned to Monica to come and sit with me.

"Are you all right?" I asked as she sat down beside me and snuggled up against me.

"Yes. In a way, I'm going to miss that place," she said with a sigh. "But I sure won't miss Campbell."

"I know how you feel."

I held her close for a while and let her be with her own thoughts. It was not going to be easy for her. The combination of losing a very good friend that she respected and admired, then losing a job that she liked and was good at all at the same time was difficult.

"Nick?"

"Yeah?"

"What are we going to do now?"

"What do you want to do?"

She leaned away from me and looked at me. I was sure that I could see a new determination growing in her beautiful cobalt blue eyes.

"I want to find the person who killed Sam, and I want to find out why he was killed," she said with a note of determination.

"Okay, then that's what we'll do."

A soft smile came over her face as she looked into my eyes. I don't think I had ever seen so much love in the eyes of a person before.

"Nick, I love you," she whispered.

She leaned toward me until our lips met. It was a long passionate kiss. One that only true love can have.

She then curled up against my side. I wrapped my arms around her and held her to me. We sat on the sofa, just enjoying the closeness we had for each other. It was like taking a time-out in a game, but what we were going to do was not a game. It was for real, and it was dangerous.

# CHAPTER FIVE

Monica and I sat on the sofa for the better part of an hour. It was comfortable having her curled up beside me. This time together gave both of us a chance to relax and clear our minds, a chance to think without pressure.

I had no idea what was going through Monica's mind, but my mind was filled with thoughts of Sam and the painting that hung on the wall in his office. I had to wonder if he was actually pointing at something on the painting in the photograph. In order to find out, I needed to see that painting again, up close. Even then, I wasn't sure if I would know or not.

Sam was clever and a little sneaky. It would be just like him to hide a very important clue to what he was doing in the painting, then hang it right in plain sight where everyone could see it. No one would even look at it twice, except for someone who was used to looking in strange places for unusual clues.

I couldn't help but think that Monica was such a person. She was always looking for clues to different things in out of the ordinary places, places where someone without her background would never think to look. It seemed to me to be part of her job.

I was another. It had been my job to look for clues in the least likely spots. And like Monica, I used technology to help from time to time. Gut feelings seemed to work well, too, at least for me.

The problem I faced now was how to get into Sam's office to get a better look at the painting. With Monica no longer employed there, getting into Sam's office was going to be a little more difficult.

"Honey?"

"Yeah?"

"Are you okay?"

"Yes, I'm fine. I think we should go to Arizona," she said with a tone of determination.

"You're probably right, but I think we have a couple of things to check out here first. We need to check out Sam's apartment, for one. I also would like to take another look at the painting in his office. We need to decide if Sam was pointing out something important in that photograph, or if he was just pointing at the painting in general."

"Do you think he is pointing out something?"

"I'm still not sure, but I get this feeling that it would be just like him to put a clue right under everyone's nose. I would like to examine the original painting again, just to be sure."

"How are we going to do that? I no longer have access to the building, except as a visitor. I doubt that I would be able to get into his office."

"What about this guard, Jerry? Do you think he would let you in?"

"I'm sure he would, but he could lose his job if he gets caught."

"You're right. I wouldn't want that to happen. I'll think of something else," I conceded.

"Maybe we should go to Sam's apartment. We might come up with something there that will make it unnecessary to see the painting again," Monica suggested.

"Like what?"

"I don't know. It was just a thought," she said almost apologetically.

This was one smart woman. She could take a problem and reduce it to its simplest form. Actually, her suggestion made a good deal of sense.

"Let's go to Sam's apartment, then we can stop off somewhere for lunch before we come back," I suggested.

"That sounds good to me," Monica said as she sat up.

I stood up and reached out to her. She took my hands and I pulled her to her feet in front of me. As I let go of her hands, she reached up and put her hands on my shoulders. I put my hands on her narrow waist. She tipped her head back and we looked into each other's eyes.

"Nicholas McCord, I love you," she said softly.

"Monica Barnhart, I love you," I replied softly, then leaned down until our lips met.

Her lips were warm and soft. As we kissed, I drew her up against me. She moaned softly as we pressed our bodies together in a passionate kiss.

"Oh, that was nice," she whispered breathlessly when we finally broke off the kiss.

"Yeah. If we do that many more times, I won't care if we leave this place at all," I said with a smile.

"In that case, we better get done what we have to do so we can do this some more," she said playfully.

"I like that idea. I like the way you think, Doctor Barnhart."

We let go of each other and got ready to leave. After closing and locking her town house door, we walked arm in arm to the garage. Once in the car, I backed it out and turned toward the street.

"Which way?"

"Head back toward downtown. His apartment is not very far from the Capitol building."

I started toward the downtown area. As I drove the little sports car, I noticed a fancy sports sedan behind us. At first I didn't think much of it, but the longer it was behind us the more I was convinced that whoever was driving it was following us.

Now, I'm not prone to paranoia, but this was beginning to bother me. I continued to watch the car in the rear view mirror. It seemed to be staying about the same distance behind us all the time while other cars were passing us or we were passing them.

I had to ask myself, if we were being followed, who could it be? The fact that the car was one of those fancy, high priced sports sedans, sort of let out the police. The next suspect that came to mind was none other than Professor William Campbell.

I guess the thing that made me think of him, was the expensive suit he was wearing when I met him earlier this morning. If he dressed like that every day, the chances were pretty good that he probably drove a car like the one behind us.

"Monica?"

"Yes?"

"What kind of car does Campbell drive?"

"I'm not sure. Why?"

"Don't turn around and look back, but I think we're being followed."

Monica looked at me, then looked out at the side mirror.

"The black sedan two cars back?"

"Yeah."

"I don't think that's Campbell's car."

"Any ideas as to who it might be?"

"I'm not sure, but it looks a little like the car that I've seen Doctor Garvey drive. Why do you think he would be following us? He was one of Sam's best friends," Monica said, the look on her face showing that she was baffled as to why Garvey would be following us.

"I don't know."

"What are you going to do?" Monica asked.

"Lose him. I don't want him to know where we're going."

I made a quick turn down a side street and hit the gas. The little sports car quickly jumped to life and sped on down the street. I looked back and saw the black sedan turn the corner behind us, but it was already two blocks back. I made another shape turn, then another at the end of that block, then a third into an alley. I raced down the alley and turned onto another street.

At this point, I was reasonably sure that I had lost the sedan. I drove several blocks and made several more turns before I continued toward the downtown area. I was sure that I had lost him, as we didn't see the car again.

Monica directed me to the apartment building where Sam's apartment was located. It was a good sized building, nine or ten stories high. I pulled into the parking lot and was able to find a parking space between two larger cars. It made the little sports car almost impossible to see from the street.

We left the car and walked into the building. We took the elevator to the fifth floor. When we got out of the elevator, Monica pointed down the hall. I followed her to the door to Sam's apartment.

When we got to the door, I looked up and down the hall to make sure that no one was around. I reached out, took hold of the doorknob and turned it. To my surprise the door was not locked. I hadn't expected it to be that easy to get into the apartment.

Monica looked at me, and I looked at her. I hesitated to open the door. At this moment, I was wishing that I had brought a gun. It didn't seem right that the door should be unlocked. Years of experience as a police office told me that this was not a good situation. We could be entering in the middle of a robbery, or we could be walking into a trap. There was no way of telling who was behind that door.

"Was Sam in the habit of leaving his door unlocked?" I asked in a whisper.

"Not that I know of," Monica replied quietly.

I motioned for Monica to stand aside, up against the wall. I looked down at the doorknob, turned it and then slowly pushed the door open. I opened it an inch at a time in an effort to be as quiet as possible. Once it was open several inches, I looked in through the crack in the door. I saw nothing, so I pushed the door open a little further.

Soon the door was opened wide enough for me to enter the room. I glanced at Monica and motioned for her to stay there. Cautiously, I stepped inside and looked around the room.

It didn't take me long to realize what had happened here. The living room was a shambles. Someone had trashed the place. It was not hard to figure out that whoever had done this was looking for something. I had to wonder if their efforts had proven fruitful, or if they had come away empty handed.

I checked out the rest of the apartment and found no one there. I returned to the door and motioned for Monica to come inside. As she stepped into the apartment, I quickly checked the hall to make sure no one had seen us, then closed the door.

When I turned around, I found Monica standing there with her hands over her mouth and her eyes as big as saucers. It was clear to me that she had not expected to find Sam's apartment like this, but then neither had I.

"My God. Who would do a thing like this?"

"Someone who was looking for something," I said as I stepped up beside her. "Are you all right?"

"Yes," she said as she continued to look around the room.

I stood next to her and began surveying the room. To the experienced eye, it was clear that whoever had trashed the place did not know what they were looking for, and they were not very experienced at searching a room. That gave me some hope that they didn't find what they were looking for. The only other reasons I could think of for someone to trash a place like this were for revenge, out of sheer frustration, or to hide something.

"What do we do now?" Monica asked as she looked around.

"We start putting this place back together as best we can."

"What?" she asked as she looked at me as if I were crazy.

"You've been here before, right?"

"Well, yes," she replied still confused by what I had suggested.

"If we put this place back together like it was, there's a possibility that you will be able to see what is missing. A small possibility, I admit. As it is now, we would have a hard time figuring out what is not here that should be. While we're doing it, we might just stumble onto something that was missed."

I could see Monica was thinking over what I had said. She looked around the room again. From the expression on her face, I think she thought I was crazy. Finally, she turned to me and smiled.

"Where do we start?"

"We might as well start right here. We'll work together. You start with the pictures. Put them back where they belong, as best you can remember. I'll work on the furniture."

Monica didn't comment. She started picking the pictures up off the floor and hanging them back on the wall. I began putting the cushions back on the sofa and chairs. As I did, I checked the underside, down in and around the seats and the cushions themselves.

"Nick, look here," Monica said.

I went to her side to see what she was looking at. On the back of a painting was a note signed by Sam Kishler. It was also dated two years ago. The note read, "To my dear friend and colleague, Monica Barnhart."

She turned the picture around so I could see it. It was another oil painting of the Superstition Mountains.

"It looks like he wanted you to have this."

"Why didn't he give it to me while he was alive?"

"I don't know, but it's clear that he wanted you to have it."

"I'll take it home with me."

"Why don't you hang it back up for now? We'll get it just before we leave."

"Okay."

As she hung it back on the wall, I went over to a desk in the corner. The drawers were open, but they had not been dumped out. From the looks of it, someone had just rummaged through them. I careful went through the drawers, checking each piece of paper. I also checked under the drawers for anything that might have been hidden there. I even checked the back of the desk in case something had been taped to it, but I found nothing.

As the room began to look picked up and put back in order, I was beginning to think that this was going to be a waste of time and effort. I glanced over at Monica to see how she was doing. I noticed that she was standing back looking at the wall.

On each side of the fireplace, she had placed the smaller framed pictures. Above the fireplace, she had returned the painting of the Superstition Mountains.

"Isn't that the same painting as the one in his office," I said as I moved up along side Monica to get a better look.

"No. It's close, but it's not the same. It was painted from a little different angle."

I studied the painting for a couple of minutes. I was not sure what I was looking for, but something came to mind.

"Why would Sam paint two pictures of the same thing?"

"I'm sure he liked it in Arizona," Monica replied as she shrugged her shoulders. "He once told me that he would like to retire there."

"No, I don't think that's the reason. I think it's because he didn't think anyone would notice the difference. One of the two paintings holds the clue to where he was working," I said, not totally convinced that I knew what I was talking about.

"Do you really think so?"

"I don't know. All I know is that if I were a painter, I would not paint the same thing twice at only a slightly different angle. I would paint it at a totally different angle so that it was clear that the paintings were different."

"I don't understand. Maybe he liked one angle better than the other."

"Possible, but I don't think that's it. Maybe one angle was better to hide a clue in," I suggested as I studied the painting.

"I don't get it."

"If you were going to paint two pictures of the same thing, wouldn't you be more likely to paint them to be either identical, or completely different? You wouldn't paint them so they looked almost alike, would you?"

"No, I guess not." Monica said after she gave it some thought.

"I think they are different for a reason. Think about this. Just suppose that Sam wanted everyone to think that the pictures were the same, but in fact, one held the starting point to where he had gone. Suppose that the small photos of the rock formations that we saw in his office are part of a photo map to where he was working. And suppose that one of these two paintings has hidden in it the starting place for that photo map."

"You would have all the pieces of the map," she said excitedly.

"Yes, you would."

"There's just one problem. Which painting is the one that shows us where to start?" she asked.

"This one," I replied confidently.

"This one?"

"Yes, this one," I replied with a smile, feeling even more confident that I was right.

Monica looked from me to the painting, then back at me. I could tell by the expression on her face that she either didn't believe me, or that she wondered how I knew it was this painting.

"Okay. How do you know that?"

"I don't, really. But think about it. Keeping in mind that Sam was sneaky, and that he was smart, very smart, right?"

"Right," she replied wondering where I was going with this.

"He was also clever. Clever, yet smart enough not to put everything in the same place."

"I get it. He put the photomap right under everyone's nose, knowing that without the starting point the pictures would be useless. By keeping the starting point here, there was little chance that anyone could put it together," she said.

"Right. There was also little chance that anyone would realized that the two paintings are different. But, there is a problem."

"What's that?"

"If we figured it out, then so could someone else."

"Do you think they have?"

"No," I replied after giving it some thought. "If they had figured it out, they wouldn't have trashed this place and left this painting behind. I think whoever did this was looking for a second copy of a map that Sam claimed he had. I don't think Sam made a copy of the map. I think he committed the map to memory, then put the original in his safety deposit box. I think the second map is the photo map he created."

"If he didn't have a second map, why would he tell me he did?"

"To get you to look for it. He trusted you. My guess is that he thought if you looked long enough and hard enough, you would figure out just what we have. And that is, the second map is this painting and the photos from his office."

"What do we do now?"

"I think we should finish picking up this place. He may have left another clue somewhere. Maybe something that would tell us that we are on the right track."

"Okay."

We once again began working on the apartment. We checked out every piece of paper we found, put every piece of furniture back where it belonged, and even made the bed after a complete search of it.

It was well past noon when we finished picking up the place. We had turned up nothing more. Monica followed me out to the living room. I dropped down on the sofa and looked up at the painting above the fireplace. There was something missing in the puzzle. If this painting contained the starting point, where was it?

Monica sat down beside me. As she leaned against me, a thought came to mind. I remembered the photo of Monica and Sam. In the photo Sam was pointing to a spot on the painting.

"Well, I'll be damned. That clever old man," I said with a slight laugh.

"What?"

"I'm not sure, but I think the painting in the photograph of you and Sam is this painting, not the one that hangs in his office. The photograph of Sam and you that was on your desk is the clue to where he was working. You had the starting point of the photomap right in front of you all the time. It was sitting on your desk in plain view where anyone could see it. All we have to do is compare it to this painting."

"You mean that he gave me that photograph so I would have what was needed to find the starting point of his photo map?" Monica said with a grin.

"Sure. Who else could he trust with it? Who else did he confide in?"

"Something I've been thinking about. The person that killed Sam, wouldn't he already know where Sam was working, maybe even know what Sam found?"

"He might, but I don't think so."

"Then wouldn't it have been better to keep Sam alive?"

"You've got a good point, certainly something to think about. The only thing I find wrong is, if someone already knew where Sam was working, why was Sam's apartment searched? Whoever's responsible for Sam's death is still missing something that is very important to them. I seriously doubt that they have found what they are looking for," I said.

"What are they looking for?"

"I don't have the slightest idea, but I'm convinced that they haven't found it yet. Now we have the chance to find it before they do. We have a map."

"What makes you so sure they haven't found it yet?"

"Gut feeling mostly, I guess. As I see it, we have two prime suspects, Campbell and Garvey. Since we already know that Professor Martin is dead, that lets him out.

"We have one secondary suspect, the guide, Juan Vasquez. At this point in time, we know of no one else who knows anything about Sam's trips into the Superstition Mountains. I'm not saying that there isn't someone else. I'm just saying that we don't know of anyone else.

"We also have two possible reasons for Sam's death. One is that he was onto something of great value, either in terms of money or in terms of historical value, and someone wants it for themselves. What that value is remains to be seen.

"The other is that he was killed to prevent him from finding it, or from telling the world about his discovery. I would be willing to bet that it's to prevent him from telling the world about his discovery. Either way, Sam is dead, and I want to know why and who did it."

"Okay. So, what's our next move?" Monica asked.

"We take your painting back to your town house. We can study it there along with the photograph of you and Sam. If the painting matches the one in the photo, we have our starting point. Once we have that, we go to Arizona."

"Do you think we can get something to eat on the way back?"

"Sure. I'm hungry, too," I replied as I stood up.

Monica stood up and walked over to the fireplace. As she reached up to take the painting down, a thought passed through my mind. I hadn't looked in the fireplace.

As soon as she had the painting off the wall and had stepped out of the way, I knelt down and looked inside the fireplace. I saw nothing that would indicate that anything was hidden there, or had been hidden there. I noticed that it was a gas fireplace, but had once been used for wood burning. My inspection of the fireplace revealed nothing.

As I stood up and brushed the dirt off my hands, I noticed that Monica was looking at me. I smiled.

"Nothing."

She nodded that she understood, then turned and started toward the door. She waited at the door while I wiped my hands on my handkerchief.

When I joined her, I listened at the door for a moment or two before I reached down and turned the doorknob. I opened the door and checked the hall. There was no one there.

I stepped out into the hall. After Monica passed me, I closed the door, making sure that it locked when I pulled it shut.

As we walked down the hall toward the elevator, I heard the bell ring indicating that the elevator was about to stop on this floor. I quickly hustled Monica into the stairwell next to the elevator. We stood leaning against the wall as we waited for the sound of footsteps to go by.

As soon as it was clear, we went on down the stairs instead of taking the elevator. Once outside the building, we put the painting in the car and got in.

As I drove out of the parking lot, I noticed a fancy black sports sedan that looked like the one that had been following us earlier. It was parked across the street. I couldn't see anyone in it. I wondered if the person in the hall was the one who had been driving it, or if it was just someone who lived there.

"Get the license number on that black sedan," I told Monica as I pointed toward the car.

I waited for Monica to find a piece of paper and pen. After she wrote the number down, we drove away.

On the way back to Monica's town house, we stopped at a drive-in and picked up a couple of hamburgers and malts. We ate them as I drove along. I kept an eye out to see if we were being followed, but I saw no one.

# CHAPTER SIX

Once we were inside Monica's town house, I set the painting on a chair and leaned it against the wall. I walked over to the other side of the room and sat down on the sofa with Monica. We sat staring at the painting while we finished eating our lunch of hamburgers and malts.

I wanted to absorb every detail of the painting I could. I wanted to get the feel of it in much the same way Sam might have. I needed to understand what Sam was trying to tell us in his painting. I was convinced that the painting held the clue to everything, I just knew it.

If I was wrong, then we had spent a lot of time and effort to get nowhere. If we couldn't find the answers in the painting, then we would never be able to find out what it was Sam was looking for, we would never be able to figure out where he had gone. We would probably never find out who killed him, either.

"I'd like to see that photograph of you and Sam," I said as I turned and looked at Monica.

"I'll get it," she replied as she stood up and left the room.

Within a few minutes, she returned with the photograph in her hand. She sat down beside me and handed it to me. I looked back and forth between the painting and the photograph until I was totally convinced that the painting in the photograph was the same as the one in front of us.

"That's the one," I said confidently as I looked at Monica.

"It is," she agreed with a smile.

"Look at the painting. Notice the slightly different color of paint at the very end of his finger? It's hardly noticeable."

"Yes. I never noticed it before. It must be the light in here that makes it show up."

"I'd be willing to bet that where the paint is a different color is the starting point of the photo map."

"I think you might be right."

"Looks like we have what we need. It's time to go to Arizona," I said with a smile as I looked at Monica.

"When do we leave?" Monica asked with a note of excitement in her voice.

"Tomorrow, but not from here. We'll leave from Milwaukee."

"Why from Milwaukee? We could get a flight out of here just as easy."

"I think were being watched. That fancy sedan that followed us earlier followed us from here. If we go to Milwaukee, we have a better chance of getting to Arizona before anyone knows we've gone."

"You're so clever," Monica said as she smiled and leaned toward me.

"I know," I replied playfully and leaned over and kissed her.

Suddenly, the doorbell disturbed our moment. Monica sat up and looked at me. I could see in her eyes that she was not expecting anyone, and that she was looking to me for directions.

"I'll take the painting into the bedroom," I said as I stood up. "Give me a minute before you answer the door."

Monica nodded that she understood. I grabbed the painting and went into the bedroom. After putting the painting in the corner behind the bed, I stepped up to the window that overlooked the parking lot. I noticed a fancy black sports sedan parked in the parking lot next to my Dodge. I could be mistaken, but it looked like the same one that had followed us this morning. I could not see the license plate to make sure.

When I returned to the living room, I found Monica standing next to the door. I nodded for her to go ahead and open the door, then I waited.

"Good afternoon, Doctor Barnhart," the well dressed man said. "I hope that I am not disturbing you."

I looked the guy over. I didn't recognize him.

"Can I help you?" Monica asked.

From Monica's response to the man, I got the impression that she did not know him, either. I didn't remember ever seeing him before.

"May I come in?" he asked politely. "I would prefer to talk inside, if you don't mind."

Monica looked back at me. I nodded, then waited as the man stepped inside the door. I noticed that he took time to look me over.

"Who are you?" I asked as I stepped closer to Monica.

"Excuse me?"

"I asked who are you?"

"I don't think that's important just yet."

"Well, I do," I said as I quickly stepped up to him, grabbed him by the collar of his sport coat, spun him around and slammed him up against the wall. I quickly frisked him for weapons.

"What do you think you're doing," he demanded, but he did not resist with any noticeable effort.

I felt something hard in the small of his back. I reached under his sport coat and removed a .38 caliber handgun from his belt.

"I'm relieving you of any temptation to get nasty," I said as I held up the gun so Monica could see it.

I turned him back around and stepped back. I kept his gun firmly gripped in my hand, ready to use if necessary. Monica stood behind me. She seemed a little shaken by it all, but then I'm sure she wasn't used to people coming into her home carrying guns.

"Now, let's get back to my original question. Who are you?"

"I still don't think that is important," he said as he straightened his sport coat and tried to look unruffled.

"Monica, call the police. They might want to know who this guy is, especially since he's carrying a gun."

Monica immediately turned and started toward the phone.

"Wait. Please, wait."

Monica stopped and looked at me for directions.

"You want to answer my question?"

He took a deep breath as he looked at me. I wasn't sure what he was thinking, but I got the impression that he was thinking about what to say.

I had no idea who he was, but he didn't strike me as a mob hood. First of all he looked a little too old. Secondly, he seemed to be a little too inexperienced for that. He sort of looked like a man who was frustrated and lost, not sure what he should do or say next. I found myself feeling a little sorry for him, but I have no idea why.

He took another deep sigh, then said. "My name is Russell Martin. Jacob Martin was my younger brother. I came here to find out if you knew anything about his death."

"Professor Martin was your brother?" Monica asked, the tone of her voice indicating that she didn't know that Jacob had a brother.

"Yes. He was also a good friend of Sam Kishler."

"We know that he was a good friend of Sam's, but what makes you think we know anything about his death?" I asked.

"Jacob told me some time ago, that Doctor Barnhart was one of Sam's closest and most trusted friends. He told me that if anything unusual happened to him or to Sam, I should find her," he explained as he looked at me.

There was something different about this man. I don't know why, but I tended to believe him. He looked like a man that was on a quest to get answers, and was not about to return home without them.

"Why the gun?"

"I would think that is rather obvious to you. Since both my brother and your friend, Sam Kishler, have been killed, a gun seemed like a good idea."

"Maybe, but not when you don't know how to use it."

"True," he admitted reluctantly.

"Why has it taken so long for you to look up Monica?" I asked.

"I've been sick and have not been able to get around until recently."

"I'm sorry about your brother, but I don't know how I can help you. What is it you want from us?" Monica asked.

"What can you tell me about the death of my brother?" he asked Monica as he looked past me.

"I'm afraid not very much," Monica replied as she stepped aside. "Please, sit down."

Russell Martin looked at me. It was clear that he was checking with me to see if it was all right. I nodded, then watched him move across the room and sit down in a chair. I followed Monica to the sofa and sat down beside her.

"I'm sorry about your brother, but all I can tell you is what Sam told me after he got back from his first trip to Arizona. He told me that your bother had gone into a cave to check it out. Since he was a geologist, they felt he was better qualified to determine if the cave was safe to enter. Sam, Professor Paul Garvey and the guide waited outside the entrance to the cave.

"Now this is where it gets a little unclear. Sam told me that he was sure that he heard a small bang, almost like a firecracker going off, just before the roof of the cave fell in. Professor Garvey, however, says he doesn't remember hearing anything other than the crashing down of the rocks," Monica explained.

"Sam heard a bang before the roof fell in?" Russell asked.

"That's what he told me, but I don't think he considered it very important. Sam sort of mentioned it rather casually as if he was not really sure about it himself."

I could see where Russell's mind was going. If there was a bang, even a small one, just before the roof fell in, then there might have been a small explosion that caused the roof to collapse. If that was the case, then it could have been murder.

My first thought was why would anyone want to kill Martin? Martin was a geologist, not an anthropologist or an archeologist. Then it occurred to me, that was the reason. As a geologist, he would have a better understanding of rock formations and how strong or weak they might be. He would be the best one to know if a cave was safe to enter, or if it needed to be reinforced before venturing into it. He might also be the best one to know about changes in the rock formations, and possibly be able to give them clues as to where certain formations might be found that could lead to what they were looking for.

"Did your brother ever tell you what they were looking for and where they were looking for it?" I asked.

"No, not really. All he told me was that he was going with his friend, Sam, and a couple of others professors to Arizona to look for evidence of some, ah, lost city or cities, or something like that. I'm afraid that I'm not really sure," he said.

"Could they have been looking for the Seven Cities of Cibola?" Monica asked, the tone of her voice showing her obvious excitement at the idea.

"I don't know, it could have been. He never really said. He only hinted at it and, I'm sorry to say, I didn't pay very close attention," he admitted.

"Well, it's clear that they were looking in the Superstition Mountains since that's where your brother was killed," Monica added.

"It's true that my brother was killed in the Superstition Mountains. But according to a letter I received from him, Sam and this Professor Garvey had a little disagreement the night before they were to leave Phoenix for the mountains."

"Did your brother say what the disagreement about?" I asked.

"It seems that they could not agree on where they should start looking for whatever it was they were looking for."

"Was it a serious disagreement or did they just discuss it?"

"I'm not really sure, but my brother said in his letter that it had put a bit of a strain on the relationship between Sam and Professor Garvey."

"If I understand you right, you're telling us that Sam and Paul Garvey were not getting along. Is that correct?" I asked in order to make sure that I understood what he was saying.

"You could say that, I guess. Although my brother didn't indicate that it was all that serious. According to his letter, Sam finally agreed to go along with Garvey's suggestion when someone else on the expedition sided with Garvey. However, from what my brother said, I got the impression that Sam was still reluctant to go along with it."

"Who was the other party that sided with Garvey?" I asked.

"I don't know. Jacob never mentioned his name. I guess I assumed it was the guide," Martin said.

"When was this letter written?"

"Only three days before my brother died."

"Three days before your brother died?"

"Yes. It was written and mailed the night before they left to go into the mountains. It was postmarked from Claypool. I looked it up on the map. It's a small town east of Phoenix, near Globe."

"Then the disagreement between Sam and Garvey was before they actually headed out into the mountains?" I asked as I thought about what he was telling us.

"That's right," Russell confirmed.

This was getting interesting. I knew from what Monica had told me that the expedition was terminated when Jacob Martin was killed. She also told me that Sam returned to Madison along with Garvey after a brief investigation indicated that Martin's death was ruled an accident by the local authorities.

It occurred to me that this was rapidly turning into an investigation of two murders, not one. It also seemed that the more we uncovered, the more it pointed to Professor Garvey as possibly having a hand in it.

I still hadn't forgotten Professor Campbell. I had seen a picture of him with Sam and Martin in Sam's office. He was still up there on the top of my suspect list. I had to wonder if he was the person who had sided with Garvey. So far, it had not been mentioned that he was even on that expedition. The question that came to mind was, had Campbell joined them later or had he left early? It was certainly something that I needed to look into.

A couple of things still bothered me. If Jacob Martin's death was not an accident, then who set the charge that caused the roof to collapse? And if it was murder, then whoever committed the murder had to have led Jacob to the cave. That would tend to point to Garvey, that is if what Martin told us was true.

"Mr. McCord, I - - -."

"How do you know who I am?"

"I'm a very rich man, sir. I make it my business to know whom I'm dealing with. I know who you are and that you are a very good investigator and police officer. I also know that I am not, which you made quite clear when you took my gun away from me with such ease.

"I'm not in the best of health and doubt that I would be able to pursue this to a final conclusion on my own. I also know that you quit your job with the Milwaukee Police Department just yesterday to come here and help Doctor Barnhart find the killer of her friend. That tells me that you are loyal to your friends, and value that friendship.

"I know that you, Doctor Barnhart, were fired from your job this morning. I'm truly sorry about that, but that tells me that you have very high values, and that you are willing to stick to your principles."

"Okay, so you know all that. What are you getting at?" I asked.

"As I said, I am not in good health. Therefore, I would like to hire the two of you to find out who killed my brother and, of course, his friend, Sam Kishler."

I looked at Monica and she looked at me. I didn't know what to say. This was not what I had expected.

"I'm curious. When did you decide that you wanted to hire us to find your brother's killer?" I asked.

"Actually, just a couple of minutes ago."

"That was sort of a quick decision."

"Yes, it was. But none the less, I'm willing to pay you for your time as well as all the expenses that you should incur in the search for the killer of my brother and of Sam's killer, of course. You could say that I want to hire both of you as private investigators. I want someone I can trust to find out the truth," he added. "And I believe that I can trust the two of you."

Having all our expenses paid would be a great help. We were both out of work and my income would only continue for a couple of months. I had no idea how long Monica would get paid before her vacation time ran out. Doing this on our own could deplete our resources very quickly.

"Suppose we take you up on your offer, what do you want out of this?" I asked.

"I want nothing except for you to find out who killed my brother and Sam Kishler, and to see that justice is done. You can keep anything you find, and do with it as you wish.

"Like I said, I'm a very rich man, but I'm in poor health. I can't be running all over the country looking for my brother's killer, although I would do that if necessary.

"And for me to accumulate any more wealth would not do a thing for me. It would not make me any healthier, or prolong my life, or anything else that means anything to me. Whatever you find, you can do with as you please. The important thing to me personally, is to find my brother's killer."

"And if it was an accident that killed your brother?" I asked.

"I'll still pay you for your time and expenses. I'm looking for the truth, that's all."

I looked at Monica, then back at Russell. From the look on his face, I was convinced that he meant what he said.

"Would you excuse us for a moment, please?" I asked.

"Certainly," he replied. "Take your time."

As I stood up, Monica stood up. I led her to the bedroom and shut the door.

"What do you think?" I asked.

"I don't know. It sounds almost too good to be true."

"Yeah. Things that sound too good to be true usually aren't true."

"I don't see as we have much choice. We're going to need money for supplies, a guide, and equipment if we're going into the mountains," Monica explained.

"I know. How do you feel about him? What does your gut tell you about him? Do you think he's for real?"

I watched as Monica thought about my questions. It was clear that she had her doubts about him, too.

"I'm not sure. Part of me tells me we can trust him, yet I have this feeling that he is not all he seems to be," she explained.

"I feel the same way about him. I'm just not sure."

"What if we run a check on him?" Monica suggested.

"Certainly a good idea. I still have some friends who could do that for us."

"What do we tell him now?" Monica asked.

"How's this? We tell him that he has a deal. He pays us ten thousand dollars up front to cover the cost of supplies, equipment, airplane fair for the two of us to Arizona and for a guide into the mountains. In the mean time, I'll have one of my friends run a background check on this Mr. Russell Martin."

"Shouldn't we require a daily fee for our services?" Monica asked. "After all, at least part of this team is a well known investigator."

I could hardly keep from laughing, but she did have a point. We were providing a service for him and he should have to pay for it.

"Sure, why not. You ready?"

"Yes," she replied.

I took her hand, leaned down and kissed her lightly on the lips. We then returned to the living room.

"We've decided to take you up on your offer. We will require an up-front payment of ten thousand dollars for expenses. This will be for supplies, equipment, a guide into the mountains and the expenses for travel to and from Arizona," I said, not sure what his reaction would be.

"Our fee is five hundred dollars a day plus expenses, that is for both of us, of course. You will get a complete accounting of all of our expenses when we return," Monica added.

"Will my personal check be good enough?" he asked without batting an eye.

"Sure, as long as we can cash it right away. We want to get started as quickly as possible," I said.

"You can cash it at the First National Bank here in Madison. I will call them and tell them to expect you," he said as he pulled a checkbook out of his inside coat pocket.

We sat there on the sofa and watched Russell write out a check. When he was finished, he handed the check to Monica. She looked at it, then showed it to me. The check was for twenty thousand dollars.

"I figure that you will need all of that. If you need more, just call me," he said as he handed me a business card. "I wish you luck in finding the killer. I would be interested in knowing when I could expect to hear from you?"

"I'll drop you a line before we start into the mountains. I doubt if we will be in contact with anyone until we come back out. I guess you'll just have to wait 'til then."

"I understand," he replied as he looked from me to Monica.

"There's just one other thing I would like to know, Mr. Martin."

"What's that, Mr. McCord?"

"Why did you follow us this morning? Why didn't you come and talk to us first thing?" I asked.

"I wasn't sure if I should approach you. I wasn't sure where you stood in all this. And I wasn't sure I wanted you to know who I was before I made up my mind on whether I should try to hire you."

"What makes you so sure now?"

"After I lost you in traffic, I made a couple of phone calls from my car. That was when I found out that you had quit your job to come here and that you, Doctor Barnhart, had been fired. I had a quick check done on the two of you, just like I'm sure you will do on me," he explained with a grin.

"I see."

"Well, I think our business is concluded for the time being. I will get out of your way so that you can get started," he said as he stood up.

We walked him to the door. As I opened the door, he turned and looked at us. He hesitated as if he wanted to say something.

"Might I make a suggestion?"

"Certainly. After all, you are paying us," Monica said.

"I might suggest that you fly out of Milwaukee if you're going to fly to Arizona. There might be someone watching you here, someone other than me."

"Good idea," I replied with a smile.

He took a couple of seconds to look at us, then he turned and walked down the hall. When he disappeared on the stairs, I shut the door and turned toward Monica.

"Do you think we did the right thing?" she asked.

"If he thinks he owns us because he paid us to find out who killed his brother, he has another think coming. We will take this as far as we can, no matter who it turns up. We were going to do it anyway. Chances are when we find out who killed Sam, we'll also find out who killed Jacob Martin."

"We're taking all the risks, he can certainly risk a little money," Monica added.

"You're right about that."

"What do we do now?"

"I have to make a call. If everything is okay, we go cash the check."

We returned to the living room and sat down on the sofa. I picked up the phone and made a call to a good friend of mine in Milwaukee. The phone rang just twice before it was answered.

"Fifth Precinct, Sergeant Wallace."

"Sergeant, this is McCord."

"Hi, Nick. How's it going?"

"Pretty good."

"I heard that you quit, that true?"

"Yeah. Say, I need a favor?"

"Shoot. What can I do for you?"

"I need a check on a Russell Martin from Minnesota."

"Russell P. Martin?"

"Yeah, I think so. You know him?"

"Sure do. He owns Swan River Manufacturing in Minnesota."

"How is it you know him?"

"I have two brother's who work at his headquarters in Minneapolis. Hell, my father worked for him most of his life. I grew up in the same small Minnesota town he did."

"What kind of a man is he?"

"He's as straight as they come. He'd give you the shirt off his back if you needed it. I don't think he spends a lot of time working at the company any more. I understand he's been in poor health for the past year or so."

"Do you know anything about his brother, Jacob?"

"Sure. Jacob was a geologist, I think. He was killed a couple of years ago in a - - ah - -cave-in. That's it. Jacob was killed in a mine cave-in somewhere in the southwest, Arizona or New Mexico, I believe."

"Can you tell me what Russell looks like?"

"He's about five-ten maybe five-eleven, weighs about one-eighty or one-ninety pounds. He might be a little lighter than that now since he's been sick. He has a full head of hair, mostly gray, and dark brown eyes. Last time I saw him he looked a little pale, but seemed to get around pretty well."

"When did you see him last?"

"At his brother's funeral in Swan River, Minnesota, about two years ago."

"Thanks, Sergeant. You've been a big help."

"Anytime, Nick. You get up this way, stop in. I'll buy coffee."

"Will do. Goodbye."

"Goodbye."

The description that Sergeant Wallace had given me fit Russell to a T. It also made me feel a little better about having him on our team.

"Well, what did he say?" Monica asked.

"He said that Russell Martin is as straight as they come. Looks like we have a job after all," I said with a grin.

"Great," she replied. "Then we're ready. We can cash the check and get ready to go."

# CHAPTER SEVEN

Monica and I sat down at the kitchen counter with a pad of paper and a pencil. We made a list of the things we would need for our expedition into the mountains of Arizona. We decided on what we should get here and what we would be better off getting when we got to Arizona.

Once the list was completed, we took the check from Mr. Russell Martin and drove to the First National Bank. The Window Teller directed us to one of the officers of the bank. He had been waiting for us just as Russell had said. The bank officer cleared the check without delay and issued us a Cashier's Check so that the money would be instantly available.

We took the Cashier's Check to Monica's bank and deposited part of it in her checking account. The rest we took in cash to go shopping for the things we would need that we could get in Madison. After getting hiking boots and clothes for the trek into the mountains, we went to the library. We spent the rest of the afternoon going over maps of the area in and around the Superstition Mountains. The maps included geological maps, maps of trails, and historically significant maps.

We had copies made of some of the maps, especially ones of the area where Jacob Martin was killed, and of the area where Sam's body was found. I was also interested in getting maps of the area immediately north of the Superstition Mountains, from Claypool west to Tortilla Flat and north to Roosevelt near Tonto National Monument as that seemed to be the area that we should take a serious look at.

By the time dinnertime had come and gone, we felt that we were as ready as we would ever be for the trip to Arizona. We got back in the car and started back toward Monica's town house.

"Are you hungry?"

"Yes," she replied.

"Would you like to stop off and get something to eat?"

"Sure. How about going to CJ's over on Spring Drive," she suggested.

"Sounds good to me. Point the way."

Monica directed me to CJ's. We were quickly seated and ordered dinner. It was a very pleasant place and the food was excellent.

After dinner, we took our time in returning to Monica's town house. When we arrived, I got the feeling that there was something wrong. I couldn't put my finger on it, but I could feel it.

"Wait here," I instructed Monica as we stepped through the door.

I looked around the room, but saw nothing unusual. I went into the bedroom and looked around. At first, I noticed nothing different there, either. Then it hit me, the painting was still in the corner of the room, but it was not leaning against the same wall where I had left it.

"Monica," I called out as I went to the window.

"Yes," she replied as she came into the bedroom.

"We've had company."

"Who?"

"I don't know, but whoever it was had a real interest in your painting.

Monica bent down and examined the painting closely. She even turned it around and examined the back, but found nothing had been disturbed.

"Whoever was here, took photographs of the painting."

"How do you know that?" Monica asked.

"Look at the covers on the bed. You can see where it was set on the bed and leaned up against the headboard. My guess is that whoever it was put the painting on the bed so he could take pictures of it, then took off when they saw or heard us coming. The balcony door is opened slightly. It was closed when we left."

"The pictures!" Monica said, a hint of panic in her voice.

I looked at Monica. I wasn't sure what she was talking about. From the look on her face, she must have realized that I didn't understand.

"The copies of the photographs from Sam's office," she reminded me.

Realizing what she was getting at, I dashed out of the bedroom and into the living room. She was right on my heels. As I looked over at the end table, I noticed the yellow envelope was missing. Without the photomap, we would probably never find out where Sam had been working.

"Damn," I blurted out in frustration. "They're gone."

Monica stepped past me to the sofa. She lifted up one of the big sofa pillows. There under the pillow was the yellow envelope, the copies still inside. She held the envelope up and smiled.

"Don't do that to me. You scared the hell out of me," I said as I caught my breath.

"I'm sorry."

"How did they get under there in the first place?"

"I hid them there while you were hiding the painting from Mr. Martin. With all that's happened, I forgot about them," she replied sheepishly.

I stepped up to her. As I put my hands on her hips, she wrapped her arms around my neck.

"I forgive you," I said as I looked into her blue eyes.

"I accept," she whispered just before our lips met.

As we kissed, I drew her up close and wrapped my arms around her. The feel of her warm lips against mine, and the feel of her body pressed against me was enough for me to want to drop this case and stay right here. After a short time, she leaned back and looked up at me.

"When are we going to leave?" she asked softly.

"In about an hour."

"We're leaving tonight?" she asked with surprise.

"Yes. Once we get packed, we're leaving for Milwaukee. From there, we'll leave on the first flight out in the morning."

"I guess I better start packing."

"Don't pack anything you can't carry on the plane. Take mostly the things we bought this afternoon. We'll get anything else we need after we get there."

"Okay, but that means I won't have anything to wear but jeans and denim shirts."

"I sure won't mind. I like the way you look in jeans," I said with a smile.

"I'm glad. It will be all you see me in for sometime," she said with a grin.

"Let's get packed. I want to leave shortly after dark. We'll spend the night at my place in Milwaukee."

I gave Monica a light kiss, then followed her to the bedroom. I laid our new carryon bags on the bed. After setting my suitcase on the foot of the bed, I began sorting out what I was going to take. When I came to the gun, I looked at it for a minute.

"Do you think we will need that?" Monica asked.

I looked up and saw Monica looking at me. I put the gun back in my suitcase.

"I would hope not, but it doesn't really matter. We can't take it on the plane anyway. They find it in a carryon bag we'll never get any further than the local police station."

Monica nodded slightly that she understood. I didn't like the idea of going into the mountains without some sort of firepower. It wasn't the four-legged creatures in the mountains I was worried about. It was the two-legged ones. They are far less predictable and far more dangerous.

There was no telling what we were getting into. This trip could prove to be very dangerous. I wouldn't mind having a small gun that no one knew I had.

Monica and I busied ourselves as we packed the things we would need. As soon as I was packed, I set my carryon case next to the door.

"Are we going to have time to take a shower before we go?"

"I plan on taking one at my place before we go to bed," I said.

"Is it okay if I take an extra change of clothes? I can leave them at your place."

"Sure."

It had already gotten dark. It was time to drive back to Milwaukee. I reached over and shut off the light on the end table. As I was shutting off the lights in the kitchen, Monica came into the room.

"Do you want me to get the light in the bedroom?"

"No. I just want them off out here. I need to find out if anyone is out there watching us."

Monica didn't say anything more. She simply stood near the kitchen counter and watched me as I moved over next to the door to the balcony. As soon as my eyes adjusted to the darkness of the room, I slowly pulled back the drapes so I could see out. I studied the parking lot and the surrounding area. At first, I didn't see anything.

Suddenly, I noticed movement in the shadow of the garage, next to a pine tree. Someone was down there.

"We've got company. Someone is hiding in the shadows next to the garage," I said as I watched for any more movement.

"What do we do?"

"I'm going down there and find out who it is."

"What do you want me to do?"

"Nothing. Leave the lights just as they are. Hopefully they will think we are getting ready for bed," I said as I started for the door.

I stopped suddenly as I remembered the gun I had taken away from Russell Martin. I reached in the drawer of the end table where I had put the gun and picked it up. I quickly checked it to make sure it was loaded.

"Be careful," Monica said."

"I will. If anything goes wrong, call the police. I'll be back in a few minutes," I said then winked at her.

I went out onto the landing and looked around. I didn't see anyone. I went around the back of the building, clear to the end. As I came around the end, I noticed that it would be impossible for anyone at the other end of the garages to see me cross the street.

After running across the street, I worked my way along the back of the garages until I was close to the end. I readied myself for an encounter.

Silently, I slipped around the corner from the back of the garage. Not twenty feet in front of me I saw a man. He was busy looking up toward Monica's apartment. I crept up behind him and placed the barrel of the gun against the back of his head. He instantly froze.

"One little move and you're dead," I whispered.

With my free hand, I took hold of the back of his shirt and turned him toward the garage wall.

"Lean against it and spread 'um," I ordered.

He did as he was told without comment. I quickly frisked him for weapons as I held the gun in the middle of his back against his spine. When I was satisfied that he was not carrying any weapons, I backed way.

"Turn around," I ordered.

I was a little surprised when I saw that he was just a college kid. From the look on his face he was scared to death that his life was going to end right here and now.

"What the hell are you doing here?" I demanded.

"I'm - - - I'm - - -."

He was so scared that he couldn't even talk, but then who could blame him. I'm sure it wasn't every day that he was looking down the barrel of a gun.

"Take a deep breath," I told him. "I'm not going to shoot you unless you try something really stupid."

I waited and gave him a chance to breathe. After a few deep breaths, he seemed to be less frightened.

"Okay. You ready to talk to me?"

"Yes, sir."

"Who the hell are you and what are you doing here?"

"I - - I'm - - - Dean Kemper. I - - - I'm - - - here to watch - - and see - - - when - - - you - - - and Doctor Barnhart leave," he said nervously.

"Who put you up to this?"

"I don't know, Mister."

"You don't know? Come on, man. You look smarter than that?"

"Honest, Mister, I don't know. I was called and told that I was to come out here and watch Doctor Barnhart's town house. I was given a number to call to report when she left. That's all I know, Mister.

"Is there anyone else watching us?"

"Not that I know of. I'm supposed to be relieved at midnight if I don't call and Doctor Barnhart doesn't leave."

"What are you getting out of this?"

"I - - - I - - -," he stuttered as he tried to decide if he should tell me or not.

"Give," I said as I pointed the gun toward him.

"I get five hundred dollars to pay off a debt."

"You must need the money pretty bad."

"I do," he admitted.

"You're a student at the university, aren't you?"

It was a guess on my part; but with all of my suspects being staff at the university and this guy being young enough to be a student, it seemed like a logical question.

"Yes."

"Now you're going to do something for me. Don't worry. You will still get your money if you cooperate. If you don't, one of my friends will be paying you a late night visit and it may be the last visitor you ever get. Do you understand what I'm telling you?"

"Yes, sir," he replied nervously.

"You're going to go down to the other end of this garage. You will wait there for thirty minutes, not one minute less. At the end of those thirty minutes, you're going to come back here and stand here until your relief comes. When he comes, you will tell him that no one left the town house. You understand?"

"Yes, sir. But what happens when they find out that Doctor Barnhart is gone."

"If you keep your mouth shut, the guy who relieves you will be the one to get the blame. If you don't keep your mouth shut, you will not get the five hundred dollars and you will get that visitor I mentioned. Is that clear?"

"Yes, sir."

"Good. Now you just go behind the garage and walk down toward the other end. By the way, I wouldn't suggest that you look back. It could be very dangerous to your health. When you get to the end, put your hands on the back of the garage and lean up against it for the full thirty minutes, not one minute less."

"Yes, sir."

"Now move."

I guided him to the back of the garage, then watched him as he walked toward the other end. When I saw him lean up against the garage, I took off across the street toward the apartment.

"Who was it?" Monica asked as I came in the door.

"Some collage student. Let's get our stuff and get out of here."

Monica picked up one of the bags and I picked up the rest. I shut off the rest of the lights and locked up her town house. We hurried down the steps to her car. Monica, got in the car while I put our bags in the trunk.

I stopped and looked toward the corner of the garage. I hesitated a moment, then went to the back corner of the garage. When I looked down the back of the garages, I saw the kid still leaning against it. I smiled to myself, then returned to the car.

It didn't take long before we were out on the Interstate. As I drove, I told Monica about my encounter at the garage.

"Nick, did you get the name of the college student?"

"It was, ah, Kemper, Dean Kemper. Do you know him?"

"Sure. He's a student of anthropology. He also works in Professor Campbell's office."

"You don't say. Is he a good student?"

"He had his problems, but he seems to be doing better now."

"What do you mean?"

"He was flunking out, but Campbell arranged for him to have a tutor. His grades have been improving lately."

"Did this tutor cost Kemper money?"

"I'm not sure, but rumor has it that Kemper had to pay the tutor five hundred dollars. I still don't know where he came up with it. It's been my understanding that Kemper was from a very poor family. I happen to know that he received a couple of grants and student aid to help him pay his tuition."

"Well, someone was paying him five hundred dollars to watch your apartment."

Monica gave me a surprised look. It was clear that she found it hard to believe that Kemper would do such a thing.

"Why would he do that, and who would have that much of an interest in us?" she asked.

"That's something I'd like to know. When Sam was in Arizona at the time Martin was killed, where was Campbell?"

"I'm not sure. I think that was about the time he flew to Washington DC. Something about a grant, I think."

"Do you remember who he was there to see?"

"No. I'm not even sure that he actually went."

"Is there some place you could find out?"

"Not tonight. There should be a record of his expenses in the administrator's office if he turned in a voucher. I have a friend who works in that office who could probably find out for me."

"Good. You can call and check on it when we get back from Arizona. Maybe you can find out where Campbell was on the days surrounding Sam's death as well," I suggested.

"You think he's involved?"

"He's involved in something, but I don't know what. I'm not absolutely sure he's involved with murder, but I'm not ready to drop him as a suspect," I replied.

As much as I was interested in where Campbell was when Martin was killed, I didn't think it was so important that I needed to know now.

Monica's little sports car purred along the stretch of Interstate between Madison and Milwaukee. The road was clear and dry, a bit different from when I went to Madison.

It was shortly after midnight when we arrived at my apartment. After parking her car in my garage, we took our things up the three flights of stairs to my apartment. Once inside, we dropped our bags by the door.

"I have a call to make. If you want to take a shower and get ready for bed, go ahead," I said as I sat down on my sofa and picked up the receiver.

"Would you like some coffee?"

"Sure," I replied as I dialed a number.

As the phone rang, I watched Monica go out to the kitchen. The phone rang several times. I was beginning to think that I was not going to reach my party.

"Hello."

"Hello. Is this Roger Thompson?"

"Yes. Who is this?"

"Nick McCord."

"Why you old son of a gun. What's up?"

"I'm coming down your way for a little while. I thought you might be able to help me with a little problem."

"Sure. You need a place to stay?"

"No. I need something else."

"Name it."

"I need a couple of small caliber pistols. Ones that can easily be concealed."

"What do you want guns like that for?"

While I explained what was going on and why I needed the guns, Monica finished making coffee. I was still talking to Roger when she came into the living room with the coffee. She set the coffee on the table and sat down beside me.

"That's all we have so far. Can you fix me up with what I need?"

"Sure can. I'll have someone meet you at the airport. You and your friend are welcome to stay with us. If you're being followed, it will make it harder for them to find you.

"Great. See what you can find out about a Juan Vasquez. He was the guide on both of Sam Kishler's trips into the Superstition Mountains. You might see if you can find out if anyone else was on that trip."

"Will do. Is there anything else I can do for you?"

"See if you can find out what the State Police have on the murder of Sam Kishler. It would be a big help."

"No problem. I can do that. I'll have it for you when you get here."

"Great. I'm looking forward to seeing you and Maggie."

"She says love and kisses. She also says that you better make time to visit us while you're here."

"We will. Give her my love."

"Will do."

I smiled to myself as I reached over and put the receiver on the cradle. I looked up at Monica. From the look on her face, I was sure that she was wondering who I had been talking to.

"That was a good friend of mine. He was a captain on the Arizona State Police up until two years ago when he had a heart attack. They forced him to retire, but he still helps out once in a while. He was a damn good investigator. He lives just outside of Phoenix with his wife, Maggie."

"Oh. I thought for a minute you were giving your love to someone else," she said playfully.

"Not a chance," I said as I pulled her close to me.

After a brief, but warm kiss, I settled back on the sofa. I picked up my coffee. We sat quietly and sipped the coffee. After a short while, Monica stood up.

"I think we should take a shower and go to bed."

Her voice was soft and sexy. It had been a very busy day for both of us. We had done all we could for now, it was time to relax.

"Would you care to join me," she added softly.

I may not be too bright, but I know a good offer when I hear one. Leaving my cup on the end table, I followed her into the bedroom. It took no time at all for us to get out of our clothes and into the shower.

Once in the shower, I found myself forgetting everything that had happened. This woman was the entire world to me. She was beautiful, intelligent and very sexy, and it was my pleasure to wash her back and have her wash mine.

After spending time in the shower, we dried each other off and crawled in between the sheets on my bed. We curled up together and drifted off into a deep restful sleep after spending some time making love to each other.

# CHAPTER EIGHT

I woke to the irritating sound of my alarm clock. Since we had gone to bed rather late, I really didn't have any great desire to get up. Monica moaned softly and rolled up against me. The feel of her warm body against me did nothing to make me want to get up, but it was time. It was time to get up and get ready for the long flight to Phoenix, Arizona.

"Mmmmmm. Do I have to get up?" Monica asked in a whisper as she snuggled up against me.

"I'm afraid so."

"If I have to get up, can I have a kiss first?"

"You can always have a kiss first."

Monica rolled up over me and wrapped her arms around my neck. I wrapped my arms around her and held her to me. She leaned down and kissed me. The feel of her naked body stretched out over me while we kissed was enough to make me want to wait for a later flight, a much later flight.

As we kissed, I slid my hands up and down her back. The smoothness of her skin and the warmth of her body was making it hard for me to want to get up. As much as I would have liked to stay here and keep touching her, we had things we had to do. One of them was to get to Arizona.

"I wish we didn't have to go," she whispered as she rose up and looked down at me."

"Me, too."

"Would you like to take a later flight?" she asked in her soft sexy voice.

"Yes, I would, but we are expected. Someone will be waiting for us at the airport in Phoenix," I reminded her. "I wouldn't want to worry Roger by being late."

Monica let out a sigh of disappointment, kissed me again and then rolled off me. I reluctantly moved to the edge of the bed and sat up. I looked back over my shoulder and took one last look at her before I stood up.

"I'll be out in a minute," I said as I went into the bathroom.

When I came out of the bathroom, Monica was gone. I went out to the kitchen and found her making coffee. She turned and looked over her shoulder at me.

"Do you mind if we have breakfast here? I don't care for the food served on the airlines."

"Sure."

"I'll be right back."

As Monica walked past me, she gave me a quick kiss and went into the bedroom while I fixed breakfast. By the time I was finished, she had returned.

"You look nice," I said as I gave her a quick once over.

"Thank you. You said you like me in jeans."

We sat down and ate our breakfast. As soon as we were finished eating, we loaded our carryon bags in her car and drove to General Mitchell International Airport. After we purchased our tickets, we had an hour to wait for our flight. I wandered off and got a couple of cups of coffee.

Being a weekday, the airport did not seem to be all that busy. We sat watching people come and go. As I watched a man walk past a display case, I noticed a reflection in the glass covered case. There was a man standing behind us. He was leaning against the wall reading a newspaper. At least that is what he was trying to convince everyone he was doing.

I doubted he knew I could see him watching us. He held the paper loosely out in front of him so that he could quickly hid behind it if I suddenly turned around.

As we watched the others pass through the terminal, the man just stood there. His reflection was too distorted by the glass for me to see who he was, but I could see enough of him to tell that he was watching us. I tend to get nervous, maybe even a little paranoid, when I'm being watched too closely.

"What's the matter?" Monica asked.

I shifted my eyes to look at her. She must have seen something in my face that worried her.

"Don't turn around, but we're being watched."

"By who?"

"I don't know, but he's standing almost directly behind me. He's wearing a dark gray jacket and black slacks, and has a local newspaper in his hands."

"Any ideas who he might be?"

"Several, but no way to prove any of them."

"What are you going to do?"

"Nothing, as long as he stays right there."

Monica looked at me with a surprised look on her face. I got the impression that she expected me to do something.

"I can't just go up to him and confront him. He may not be watching us at all. He might be watching someone else," I said in an effort to ease her worry.

We sat quietly for almost an hour before the announcement of our flight came over the address system. It was time to board the plane. We got up and picked up our carryon bags.

As we filed along the line toward the door, I glanced back toward the man. He continued to watch us until I lost sight of him. It did not look like he was going to follow us onto the plane.

We found our seats. Monica took the seat next to the window. I watched each passenger as they boarded. The man did not board the plane. I looked to see if someone else might be watching us, but I saw no one else that seemed to be taking an interest in us.

"Did he board the plane?" Monica asked.

"No."

"Who do you think he was?" Monica asked.

"If I had to guess, I would say it was probably someone hired to make sure we got on the plane."

"You mean Russell Martin?"

"It's not him, but could be someone who works for him. Maybe he's just looking after his investment," I said with a grin in the hope of relieving her tension.

My answer seemed to be acceptable to her. As the cabin door closed, we fastened our seat belts. The plane started to move away from the terminal. Monica reached over and put her hand over mine.

"This will be a good time to relax. I don't think we will have much time to relax once we get to Phoenix," I said.

"You're probably right. What are you going to do?"

"I'm going to spend some time studying the maps we got from the library."

As soon as we were airborne and well on our way, I took the maps out of the side pocket of my carryon bag. I spread them out on the foldout table from the back of the seat in front of me.

The first map was of the area where Professor Martin had died, or should I say, was killed. From the looks of the map, it looked like it was fairly rugged terrain. There were several trails into the area, but nothing that could be called a road. That would mean that everything they took with them must have been packed in, probably on horseback.

I spent a long time studying each and every detail of the topographical map. The details of the map were excellent, but it was still not as good as seeing it in person. There was no doubt in my mind that we were going to have to go into that area. I wanted to know as much about it as possible, it could save our lives.

When I was finished studying the first map, I went on to the second. This one was of the area around Castle Dome where Sam's body had been found. I immediately noticed that there were several roads into the area. It was clear that they were roads that would require a four-wheel drive vehicle, but roads never the less.

It didn't take me long to find the water hole at the base of Castle Dome where Sam's body had been found. The map indicated a picnic area, or a place where one could camp near the water hole. I assumed that was where the jeep tour group had spent the night.

I began to study the map as I had the other. I noticed that there were several small symbols on the map, a shovel and pick crossed to form an X. A quick check of the map's key told me that the symbols marked the approximate location of known mines. If there were that many known mines, I had to wonder how many unknown mines there might be.

I tipped my head back and closed my eyes. My mind tried to think of Sam and what he was really after. I tried to put myself in his shoes.

If Sam had the same maps I had, and he probably did, he probably would not have given the mines indicated on the map a single thought. Mines located on a map that is available to anyone would be the first mines searched by everyone. Sam would have been looking for something that was not so obvious, something that had remained hidden for centuries. The fact that the area where his body was found was saturated with mines would surely indicate that the area had been gone over a number of times over the years by miners, treasure hunters and just plain sightseers.

It became very clear to me that Sam wasn't looking for anything near Castle Dome. His body was dumped there so it would be found, and so that it would be believed that he had been working in that area. It was clear to me that whoever killed him, wanted his body found. Why, I wasn't sure, but probably to keep the authorities from snooping around the area where he had actually been working. That would explain why his body was not just dumped down some deserted mine shaft in the mountains where it might never be found. The only question remaining was where had he been working?

My thoughts were disturbed by the sudden change in the pitch of the jet engines. I opened my eyes and looked at Monica. She was smiling at me. I realized that I had fallen asleep for at least part of the flight.

"We're almost there. Did you find anything interesting?" she asked.

"Nothing I can be sure of until we get there. I hope everything is ready. I want to get into the mountains as soon as possible."

"What do you think you found?"

"I'm not sure, but I have an idea where Sam was trying to get. It just came to me."

"Where?"

Just then a bell rang and the seat belt light came on. We put on our seat belts before I answered.

"I believe he was trying to get to an area on the northeast or north side of the Superstition Mountains. An area that looks to be pretty rough and hard to get to. The painting and the photograph of you and Sam are the keys to where we are to start. The other photos tell us where to go from there," I explained.

"But they don't show us what he was looking for."

"That's true, but I think that Sam was sure you would know, once you got there."

"Me?"

"Yes, you."

"But I have no idea what he was looking for. If I don't know what he was looking for, how am I supposed to find it?"

"I don't know, but I have a feeling that we will find out when we get there, wherever "there" is."

"I'm glad you're so sure, because I haven't got the foggiest idea."

"Neither do I, but we just have to trust that Sam knew what he was doing."

"Maybe he did, but it got him killed," she remarked.

She was right. It had gotten him killed. I had to wonder what it was that he had found, or what it was that he was getting so close to finding that someone found it necessary to kill him.

The thought came to mind that he might have been killed to prevent him from discovering something that someone didn't want him to find. This was not the first time I had thoughts like that, but it was becoming a very real possibility.

Legend has some basis in fact. I remember Monica telling me that. It is believed by some that the Superstition Mountains are watched over by spirits or ghosts. I never have been a great believer in spirits or ghosts, but there could be a small group of people living in the mountains who make it their life's work to keep certain things a secret from the rest of the world. I knew it was a long shot, but it was possible.

The other thought that came to mind was that Sam had found what he was looking for, but the person who killed him wanted it left hidden until things cooled down. Then that person would find it and claim the discovery, thus getting the credit for the find and the glory. That seemed to me to be a more likely scenario. There was even a little evidence to support that theory, namely the jewelry that was found in Sam's pocket. It indicated that Sam had found something. Just what he had found was yet to be determined.

My thoughts were again disturbed before I had a chance to talk to Monica about the fax she had received from the Arizona State Police. Only this time I was interrupted by the slight jar of the plane as its wheels touched down on the runway. I leaned over and looked out the window toward the terminal. I wondered who would be waiting for us. I knew that Roger had made arrangements for someone to meet us at the airport, but who else might be there to watch what we do, and where we go.

As soon as the plane had stopped at the terminal, everyone seemed to be in a hurry to get off. Monica and I remained seated until the crowd cleared out a little.

Once the crowd had thinned out, we got our bags and worked our way to the front of the plane. We were the last passengers to get off the plane. As we walked into the terminal, I looked around. I halfway expected to see someone carrying a sign with our names on it, but I saw no one with a sign. What I did see were two uniformed officers of the Arizona State Police.

As we came to the end of the rail, one of the officers stepped forward.

"Excuse me, sir. Are you Nick McCord?" the officer asked.

"Yes," I replied.

"I'm Sergeant Edwards of the Arizona State Police. I've been instructed to personally take you to Captain Roger Thompson's home. He asked us to welcome you to Arizona. He also asked us to see to it that you arrive safely, and make sure that you are not followed."

"Thank you, Sergeant. This is Monica Barnhart, my partner."

"Nice to meet you, ma'am."

"Nice to meet you, Sergeant," she replied with a smile.

"We have a car waiting. This way, please."

Monica and I followed the sergeant out of the reception area and through a side door. Just outside was an Arizona State Police car. The other officer took our bags and put them in the trunk, while the sergeant held the door.

"I certainly didn't expect the royal treatment, but I can't say I mind," I commented.

"Captain Thompson said that you are a personal friend of his, and he wants nothing to happen to you while you are here. He also said that he has information that might help with your investigation of the death of that College Professor from Wisconsin."

"Do you know what that information might be?" Monica asked.

"No, ma'am. He just told us to deliver you directly to him."

As soon as Sergeant Edwards got in the car, we were off. It was about a forty-five minute drive to a rather nice middle class neighborhood. Edwards pulled into the driveway of a Spanish style home and stopped.

Before I could get out of the car, I saw Roger come out the front door. He had a big grin on his face. I also noticed that Maggie was following him.

"Damn, it's good to see you again," Roger said as he stuck out his hand.

"You're looking pretty good," I replied as I shook his hand.

I let go of his hand and turned toward Maggie.

"Maggie, you're as beautiful as ever," I said as I wrapped my arms around her and kissed her on the cheek.

"And you're as full of it as ever, Nicholas," she replied with a big grin. "And who is this?"

"Maggie, this is my dear friend and partner, Monica Barnhart."

"Welcome to Arizona, Monica," Maggie said. "Any friend of Nick's is a friend of ours. Please come in out of the sun."

I watched as Maggie and Monica walked toward the house. I was glad that they seemed to hit it off so well, but then everyone likes Maggie.

After Roger and I took the bags from the officers, Roger released them to other assignments. I walked with Roger to the house and went inside.

"Put your bags in the bedroom, the second door on the left," Maggie said as she pointed toward the hall.

I took the bag from Roger and carried them to the bedroom. When I returned to the living room, I found Monica and Maggie sitting on the sofa getting acquainted. Roger was in a chair across from them, just listening. Roger looked up at me.

"Have a seat, Nick."

"I'm sorry that you couldn't come to visit under better circumstances," Maggie said.

"I'm sorry, too," Monica said.

"Roger, what were you able to find out?" I asked.

"Your Professor Kishler was killed with two shots from a .30 caliber rifle. It looks as if the first shot was from some distance, maybe as much as two hundred yards. The second shot was up close and personal, not more than a few inches. We found powder burns on his shirt. We examined the rifle carried by the man who had been scheduled to be his guide, but it was the opinion of the crime lab that the guide's rifle did not do the shooting."

"Was anyone else in the group carrying a rifle?"

"What group? Sam Kishler was in the mountains alone."

"What? I thought there were two or three others with him." I said.

"No. He had a guide, but he fired his guide just before he started into the mountains."

"Monica was told that he was not killed where his body was found. Any idea as to where he was shot?"

"No. Not so far."

"A piece of jewelry was found on Sam, a very old piece of jewelry. The police sent me a fax photo of it. I was supposed to tell them everything I could about it," Monica said.

"Yes, I know. I was the one who gave them permission to send it to you," Roger said. "What can you tell me about it?"

"Not much, I'm afraid. To be sure, I would have to see the piece," she apologized.

"I can arrange that."

"I am sure of one thing. It is very old. It looks like something that could have been made by an ancient people who lived in this region around the time of the first Spanish expeditions into Arizona and New Mexico, in the 1540's. Of course, I can't be sure until I examine it."

"I'll see to it that you get it," Roger assured her.

"Were you able to find out anything else?" I asked.

"I did find out something that was interesting. It seems that the guide that was hired to lead the expedition two years ago when Professor Martin died in the cave, was the very same guide hired for Kishler's last trip into the mountains. The guide he fired."

"Yeah?"

"It wouldn't be unusual to use the same guide, would it?" Monica asked.

"No, not normally. But you see most people who are not familiar with the Superstition Mountains would hire someone locally, someone with a reputation for knowing the mountains. We were able to find out that this guide was personally selected for Doctor Kishler by someone who called long distance."

"I don't understand. You mean, someone asked for this particular guide?" I asked as I was confused by what had been going on.

"Right. The guide service advised the caller that they had better qualified guides, guides that knew the region better, but the caller insisted on using that particular guide."

"Any idea who made the call?"

"The guide service said that the person who called never mentioned his name. A check with the telephone company revealed that the call had been made from a pay phone in Middleton, Wisconsin. That was all we were able to find out about it."

"That's a suburb of Madison," Monica announced as she looked over at me.

"Do you know anyone who lives in Middleton?" I asked Monica.

"No," Monica replied after thinking about it for a moment.

"Have you run a background check on the guide?" I asked Roger.

"We sure did. He has a record as long as your arm for assault and robbery, but only a couple of minor convictions. He was never convicted of anything very serious."

"Have you tried to talk to him?"

"We did talk to him right after we found Kishler's body. We've tried to talk to him again, but he's an Apache and lives on the Fort Apache Indian Reservation along the Salt River. No one there is willing to tell us where he is or how we can find him. They tend to protect their own."

"Where was this guide when Sam was killed?" I asked.

"Like I said, Sam fired the guide before he went into the mountains. As far as we've been able to determine, the guide spent a few days in the mountains with another party. We believe that after we questioned him and checked his rifle, he went back to the reservation."

"Do you think Sam knew that the guide was not to be trusted?"

"He might have, but there's no way to know for sure," Roger replied. "We do know that Sam rented several animals, two pack animals and one to ride."

"Did you ever find the animals?"

"Yeah. They showed up late one night at the ranch where he had rented them. No one seems to know how they got there. We suspect that they had been turned loose not far from the ranch and simply found their way back to the ranch where there was food and water for them."

"You said that the guide was with another party after Sam had fired him. Do you know who the party was?

116

"No. He wouldn't say."

"So you really only have his word for it?"

"That's right."

So far it seemed that we had a lot of information, but none of it could be proven. It was also very little help other than to make us aware of the need to be cautious. We spent the next few hours visiting and discussing what information and what evidence they had been able to gather up to this point.

That evening, Roger had the piece of jewelry that had been found on Sam brought to his house. Monica examined it and came to the conclusion that it was, in fact, a very old piece of jewelry typical of that made by an ancient Indian tribe that had once lived in the area.

This was the first solid piece of evidence we had that Sam may have made an important find. The major problem was that we had little idea as to where he had found it, and if what he found was still there.

By the time nightfall had come, we had talked ourselves hoarse. Roger and I had sat down in his den and laid out the maps, the photographs and a list of findings from the police investigation. He had already made all the arrangements for our trip into the mountain, including packhorses and all the gear we would need.

Roger also arranged for a guide that was often used by the police to find lost hikers. The guide was also used to help in investigations that took the police into the mountains. Roger assured me that the guide could be trusted, and that he was an excellent tracker, guide and marksman. I was hoping that we would not need his skill as a marksman, but was glad to know he could be trusted and had such skills.

"By the way, I have what you asked for," Roger said as he stood up and walked across the den.

At first, I wasn't sure what he was talking about. When he took two small pistols out of a drawer in a cabinet, I quickly remembered.

"Does Monica know how to use one of these?"

"I'm not sure," I replied.

"I'll give you one for her, just in case. This little .25 caliber automatic should suit her just fine. I got a .38 caliber for you."

"Great," I replied as he handed them to me.

I quickly checked them to make sure they were loaded.

"These will be fine," I said.

"Good. I hope you don't have to use them, but I feel better knowing that you have them."

"Thanks."

"I think you and Monica had better get some shut-eye. You'll be leaving early."

"Right."

I followed Roger out of the den and into the living room. We found Monica sitting with Maggie on the sofa.

"Maggie, it's been great to see you again, but I think we should get some sleep. We are leaving early in the morning."

"I understand. Will you be able to stay a little while after you get back?"

"I sure hope so."

"Good, then I'll say goodnight."

As soon as everyone had said goodnight, Monica and I went to the bedroom. We undressed in silence. I don't know what was on Monica's mind, but the trip into the mountains was on mine.

I couldn't help but think about how dangerous this was going to be. Two people had already been killed. They had some idea of what they were looking for, we didn't. We were not only looking for what they had been looking for, we were looking for the person who had killed them.

We crawled into bed. Monica immediately curled up beside me, but tonight was different. I could feel the warmth of her beautiful body just as before, but tonight it did not erase the thoughts of tomorrow from my mind.

"I love you," she whispered.

I didn't answer her. Instead, I squeezed her tightly against me. I was worried about her. What business did I have taking her into those mountains? But on the other hand, what choice did I have? There was no way she would stay behind. Deep down inside me, I really wanted her with me.

We laid in silence for a long time, wrapped in each other's arms. Our thoughts made it difficult for us to find sleep, but sleep finally did come.

# CHAPTER NINE

I didn't need an alarm clock to tell me when to get up. I was up with the sun. This was going to be a big day for us. It could be the start of what might prove to be an interesting as well as a dangerous trip. We had no idea what we were getting into, but whatever it was we were in it together. We had made all the preparations that we could. Now it was time to take the first step.

Monica was down the hall in the bathroom while I was getting dressed. I had a lot on my mind as I sat on the edge of the bed putting on my hiking boots. When she returned I noticed that she was dressed except for her boots. I needed to talk to her about the gun I had for her.

"I've been meaning to ask you. Do you know how to handle a gun?" I asked as she sat down on the edge of the bed beside me.

At first she didn't say anything or even look at me. She simply bent down and picked up one of her boots. She turned and looked at me as she slipped her foot into the boot.

"Yes," she replied softly. "My father taught me to shoot a long time ago."

I reached behind me and held out the .25 caliber pistol to her.

"I want you to carry this. I don't want you to let anyone know you have it. Do you understand?"

She looked at the gun in my hand for a moment before she reached out and took it. I watched her as she checked it to make sure it was loaded. It did a lot to make me feel better about her having a gun. At least she showed me that she knew how to handle a gun safely.

She slipped the gun inside her loose fitting blouse and tucked it in her belt. She didn't say anything until after she finished putting on her hiking boots. When she was ready, she looked at me.

"Nick?"

"Yeah, honey."

"Do you think I will need it?" she said as she looked at me with those beautiful blue eyes.

"I don't know, I sure hope not. But if it makes you feel any better, I feel better knowing that you have it."

She hesitated for a minute while she watched me strap on a leg holster and put the snub nose .38 caliber pistol in it. As I pulled my pant leg down over it and straightened up, she looked up at me.

"I know I feel better knowing that you have one," she commented softly.

We stood up together. I reached out and took hold of her hand. I wanted to say something profound, but nothing came to mind. She stepped up to me, reached up and put a hand on my cheek as she looked into my eyes. I leaned down and kissed her lightly on the lips.

"You know you don't have to go," I said almost hoping that she would take the hint.

"I do have to go. You said it yourself. I'm the one who will know what we are looking for when we see it."

"I guess I did," I admitted.

Suddenly, there was light knock on our door. We could hear a quiet voice from the other side that caused us to smile.

"Breakfast is ready."

I reached over and opened the door. Maggie looked a little surprised. I got the impression that she was not even sure we were up.

"We'll be right there," I said.

She didn't comment. She smiled, nodded, and went on down the hall toward the kitchen. As soon as she was out of sight, I turned back to Monica.

"Ready for breakfast?"

"Yes."

I took her hand and walked with her to the kitchen. When we entered the kitchen, we found Roger sitting at the table. On the table was a platter of eggs, bacon and sausage. There was also a small plate stacked with toast. As I pulled out a chair for Monica, I noticed that there was juice already poured.

"Sit down and eat up. It may be awhile before you get to eat a meal without dirt and bugs in your food."

"Roger!" Maggie said with a disgusted tone in her voice.

"Well, it's true. Camping out and cooking over an open fire usually means dirt in your food, and bugs," I agreed.

"I'll be fine," Monica assured Maggie. "I remember what it was like when I was a little girl and my whole family would go camping."

"An outdoor girl, hey, Nick."

"I sure hope so," I replied with a grin.

As I put some food on my plate, I found my mind thinking about this trip. It was certainly not going to be a family camping trip.

"What are you so quiet about, Nick?" Roger asked.

"The mountains," I replied.

The room went quiet. I was sure that all the talk up to now had been to help ease the strain. We were going into the mountains not only to find a lost treasure, but to find a killer as well. There was nothing fun about the trip.

Nothing more was said. Everyone sat quietly and ate. As I drank my coffee, I realized that this could be the last meal that Monica and I might have together under a roof.

I was used to investigating things, but I was not used to this. I knew the dangers that lurked around corners, and from windows and behind doors. But there were no windows or doors where we were going. I was out of my element here. It was not at all like the city. I had to admit, if only to myself, that I was a little nervous.

I was startled by the sound of the doorbell. It had caught me off guard causing me to spill a little of my coffee.

"Looks like your guide is here," Roger said as he pushed back his chair.

I looked at Monica, then toward the living room. I could not see the front door, but I heard Roger invite someone in. When he returned to the kitchen, he was with a short man with wavy black hair and dark skin.

"This is Roberto Martinez. Roberto, this is my friend from Wisconsin, Nick McCord and his friend, Monica Barnhart."

I stood up and reached out a hand to him. He reached out and shook my hand. I immediately noticed that his handshake was firm, a good sign to me.

"Glad to meet you, Roberto."

"I have heard about you, and you too, ma'am," he said as he nodded a greeting to Monica. "Are you ready to get started?"

"Would you like something to eat first?" Roger asked.

"No, thank you. I've already eaten."

"Well, I guess we're ready to go," I said.

We got up from the table. Everyone followed Roberto out of the house except me. I went back to the bedroom to get our bags. When I returned, I found Monica waiting for me next to the jeep. I tossed our bags into the jeep and jumped in the back.

Monica sat in the passenger's seat while Roberto climbed in behind the wheel. We waved goodbye to Roger and Maggie as Roberto pulled away from the curb.

A quick look around the jeep told me that the only bags or supplies in the jeep were the bags that belonged to Monica and me. I watched Roberto as he drove through traffic with the ease and skill of a city born man. He headed east out of town toward the mountains.

"Say Roberto, you don't have any supplies in here," I said.

"Our supplies and horses are waiting for us at a base camp in the Superstition Mountains. Captain Thompson made arrangements for us to be met at the same base camp the professor that was killed had left from the last couple of times he was here."

"Oh," I replied feeling a little stupid.

"Excuse me for asking, Mr. McCord, but do you know how to handle a rifle?"

"Yes. Why?"

"I wasn't sure. Mr. Thompson asked me to make sure you had ample firepower. He told me that we might run into problems getting to where you need to go."

"That's probably true."

"I have a pistol and holster for you, and a rifle. My partner and I will be armed as well," he said with confidence.

Monica looked back over her shoulder at me. I could see the worried look on her face, but I reassured her that everything was all right by winking at her. I also reached out and put my hand on her shoulder.

After a number of miles, Roberto turned off the highway onto a dirt road. He drove down the road at a pretty good clip. Off in the distance I could see the Superstition Mountains looming up from the desert floor. I had to admit that they were an impressive sight. Just the name of them reminded me of some of the stories I had heard about people going into the mountains and never returning.

Roberto began to slow down, then turned off onto another road, if you could call it that. Actually, the road was more like a two-lane cow path. The going was slow now. The jeep bounced along as we followed each twist and turn in the trail. I found it necessary to hang on.

We went down through a dry creek bed and up the other side. We then followed another narrow trail. It was just wide enough for the jeep in some places as we wound our way higher and higher above the desert floor. In some places the trail dropped off fifty to sixty feet on one side and went almost straight up on the other. I sure hoped that Roberto knew where he was going.

As we came around a bend, it sort of flattened out. Up ahead, about a hundred yards or so, was a small grove of trees surrounded by thick grass. It was like an oasis in the middle of the rocky desert. It was then that I noticed several horses back in the shade of the trees.

I saw a man come out of the trees as we pulled to a stop. He was a tall man carrying a rifle in his hand. I also noticed that he had a six-gun on his hip.

"This is our base camp," Roberto said. "From here we go on horseback."

I jumped out of the jeep and then helped Monica out. We walked around in front of the jeep to greet the man.

"Mr. McCord, this is Bill Roth of the Arizona State Police. Bill, this is Nick McCord and Monica Barnhart."

"Nice to met you," he said politely, then turned and looked at Monica. "I didn't know we were going to have a woman on this expedition."

"Is that a problem, officer?" Monica asked.

"No, ma'am. I just didn't know."

Monica looked at me. I was sure I could see that she didn't like the way the officer had looked at her, or his comment. Even I picked up on a hint of sarcasm in his voice at the thought of having a woman on the trip. I was sure that Monica had, too.

We followed Bill and Roberto to the base camp. It was clear that the area had been used as a campsite several times before, which would be expected since I was told that Sam had used it as a jumping off point of previous trips into the Mountains.

Roth went to a tent and returned with another rifle.

"This is for you. It's from Captain Thompson," he said as he held out the rifle.

I thanked him, then took the gun and leaned it against a tree. I took notice of the fact that I was not given a side arm as Roberto had said that I would get. It didn't bother me too much as I already had a pistol, but I wasn't about to let anyone know about it. We sat down on a log near where a fire had been built.

"How long have you been here?" I asked Roth.

"I've been here since late yesterday afternoon," Bill said.

"I take it you know this area pretty well," I said.

"As well as anybody, I guess."

"I think it would be a good idea if we get our maps out so we can show you the areas where we want to go."

"Okay, but I have some government maps of the area. We can use them," Bill suggested.

"Great, they're probably more detailed than the ones I have, anyway."

Officer Roth went to the tent again. He returned with a couple of maps. After laying the maps out on a table, we gathered around as he pointed out our location.

"We are here. Where is it you want to go?"

I looked over at Monica. She looked at me, then turned and looked at the map.

"We want to go up here, then over here," she said as she pointed at two separate locations on the map.

"That one is easy. We can pack into that area on horses," Roth replied as he pointed to the first location on the map.

"But the other one is pretty rough," he continued as he pointed at the second location.

"Are you saying that we can't go into that area?" I asked.

I knew I made it sound like a challenge, but that area was very important to us. That was the area that we believed Sam had been working in, and may have been where he was killed. It was in that area that we really hoped to find the trail that was pictured in the photo map Sam had left. We also hoped to find the evidence we needed to prove that Sam had been killed there. We also hoped to find evidence that would point us to his killer.

"No. It's not impossible to get into that area. All I'm saying is that it will not be easy. We will have to pack in everything we need, including water. For the last five miles or so we won't be able to take the horses. We'll have to carry supplies," Roth explained.

"I see. There are no springs in that area, no water supply of any kind?" I asked.

"Not that we know of. There may be a couple of bathtubs in the area, but if it hasn't rained in several days they could be dried up," he said as he looked at me.

"Bathtubs?" I asked.

"Yeah. They're what we call hollowed out places in the rock formations, hollowed out by the wind and sand. When it rains they fill up with water. They sort of look like a bathtub," Roberto explained.

"Has it rained recently?" Monica asked.

"Yes, but it's hard to tell if it rained enough to fill the bathtubs, or if it even rained where they are. We had a pretty good rain in Phoenix a couple of days ago, but I'm not sure it rained very much out here. It was sort of spotty. Then there is the problem that we have no idea where they might be located. They are not marked on any map I know of," Roberto added.

"It looks to me like we should head out for the first location with the horses. After you have checked out that area, we can take the horses as far as possible, then go the rest of the way on foot," Roth suggested.

It sounded like the best plan to me. I looked at Monica to see if she agreed. She nodded slightly indicating that it was okay with her.

"Okay. That sounds like a plan. When do we start?"

"As soon as we get our supplies packed on the horses," Roth said.

"Good. What do I do? I'm not a horseman, although I have ridden a horse once."

Not being very familiar with horses, it was left to me to do some of the little things. After I had helped to take down the tents and roll them up, I helped packed what I could and helped get the packhorses ready.

As soon as we were ready, I put my rifle in the scabbard and then mounted up. I did manage to mount up without making a fool of myself. I just hoped that the horse knew what it was doing because I sure didn't.

Once we were all mounted, Roth led off. He had a packhorse in tow. He was followed by Monica, then me. Roberto pulled up the rear with the other packhorse.

The sky was blue and full of sunshine. It was also warm with the possibility of getting down right hot as the day went on. There was very little breeze to help cool the rays of the sun.

Our pace was slow, but steady. I noticed that we were gradually climbing in altitude. As I looked back over my shoulder, I could see part of the Phoenix skyline in the distance just before we rounded a corner.

"Pretty sight isn't it," Roberto called out to me.

"Yes, it is."

"We don't get to see it like that very often with all the smog. You should really see it from here on a clear night."

I nodded at him, then turned back around. I had to wonder if I would ever get the chance to see it at night.

As we rode along the trail, it seemed to be getting narrower. It was beautiful country, but I was not enjoying it. My mind was too busy thinking. It was hard for me to judge how far we had gone, and if we were going where Roth had said he would take us.

"Hold up a minute," I called out and drew the reins back to stop my horse.

I swung my leg over the saddle and stepped down. I flipped the stirrup up over the saddle and made it look like I was checking the girth. When I glanced toward Roth, I noticed that he had simply stopped and was looking back

toward me.    He made no effort to move toward me.
However, Roberto quickly came to see if he could be of any
help.

"Do you know anything about Roth?" I asked Roberto
quietly as he stood beside me checking the girth.

"No, not really.  I only met him today," he replied in a
whisper.

"You've never met him before?"

"No.  He was assigned to this duty because he knows the
area."

"Is everything all right," Roth called out.

"Yeah.  I just need to make a little adjustment," I yelled
back.

I watched him turn around.  I noticed a disgusted look
come over his face just before he turned his face away from
us.

"By who?"

"I don't know.  He's from somewhere around Flagstaff,
I'm told."

"I trust you.  You were hand picked by Thompson.  I
trust Roger, as I'm sure you do.  But I'm not as confident
about Roth.  I don't know what it is, but something about him
doesn't sit right," I said.

"Thompson said that it was going to be a dangerous
mission.  I trust no one," Roberto said.

"Good idea.  We better get going."

As Roberto walked back to his horse, I stepped in the
stirrup and swung my leg over the saddle.  As I settled in, I
noticed Monica watching me.  I'm sure she knew something
was not right, but she did not let on.

Once again we started out along the trail.  I kept my eyes
open and moving around.  We were spread out enough that
we could easily be ambushed.  I also noticed that there was
no place for us to take cover if we were attacked.  That
didn't set well with me.

We stopped near a small water hole for lunch. We gave the horses a bit of grain and let them have a drink. After we had our lunch, we were back in the saddle again and started along the narrow trail.

We stopped several times during the afternoon to rest the horses and to give them water. It was not an easy ride, which could have accounted for the silence among us. I did notice that Roth kept looking back at me. It was as if he thought he knew me, but couldn't place me. I knew that wasn't the reason, but I didn't know what the reason was. Maybe, it was his way of sizing me up. Seeing if I had what it takes to make a trip like this. Maybe it was more than that. I just didn't know what was going on in his head.

Making the trip was not much of a concern to me. I knew I had what it took. I even had confidence in Monica. My worry was whether or not we would end up like Martin and Sam, dead.

We continued to travel along the ridge, slowly continuing the long climb up into the mountains. The trail was very crooked. It wound around large outcroppings of rock, down through dry creek beds, and up over rocky ridges. The one thing you could say about it was that it was not a boring ride, nor was it an easy ride for this city boy.

The only things I saw all day long were a few jackrabbits and several quail. Otherwise, there was nothing but cactus, cactus and more cactus. As the day went on, I noticed that we were seeing less and less cactus, but more and more rocks.

The only sounds I heard were those of a few quail scurrying through the underbrush and an occasional bird taking flight. Even those sounds disappeared as the vegetation grew scarcer.

As our shadows grew long, I was beginning to feel tired and saddle weary. I wasn't used to being in a saddle all day. I knew Monica wasn't, either.

"Just a little further and we will get to a good place to spend the night," Roth announced as if he knew what I was thinking.

"Great," I heard Monica say.

After about another half-hour, we came around an outcropping of rocks, turned and went behind some boulders, then out onto a flat level area. It was amazing. There were several trees, and a small area of lush green grass. Somewhere in this beautiful spot there had to be water. Nothing grew around here without it.

"This is Black Rock Springs," Roberto said as he drew up beside me. "Not many people have ever been here."

"This is beautiful," Monica announced as she stepped out of the saddle.

We all got out of the saddle. I stretched in the hope of getting a little of the stiffness out of my back and backside.

"We'll be spending the night here. Tomorrow we will get to the first location you pointed out. There are several caves and a few mines in that area," Roth said.

"Are you familiar with the cave that Professor Martin lost his life in?" I asked.

"Yes, sir. I was one of the officers who was there to retrieve Professor Martin's body," Roth replied.

"Oh," Monica replied.

"The two of you can relax for awhile. Roberto and I will set up camp and fix dinner. There's a spring right over there if you would like to wash up a little," Roth said as he pointed off toward a big tree. "The water is safe to drink."

"Thank you," I said and took Monica by the hand.

We walked over to the spring and splashed some water on our faces. The cool water felt good.

"Is everything all right?" Monica asked in a whisper as she dried her face.

"So far. I find it interesting that Roth didn't mention that he knew where the cave was when we pointed out the location on the map. He waited until now to tell us."

"Do you think he had something to do with Martin's death?"

"No, not yet anyway. But I plan to keep an eye on him. I can't say that I trust him."

The rest of the evening was quiet. We looked over the map with Roth. He pointed out where we were going in the morning and about how long it would take. He also pointed out the location of the cave where Martin was killed.

It had been a long day for all of us. As soon as it was dark, Monica and I curled up in our sleeping bags. Monica fell asleep very quickly, but I only pretended to be asleep. I laid quietly watching Roth. It wasn't long before he laid down and went to sleep. I noticed Roberto had leaned up against a rock and fell asleep there.

I laid there on my bedroll looking up at a sky full of stars. There were more stars than I could count. It was beautiful. It was also very quiet, except for the heavy breathing of those who were already sleeping.

It wasn't long before I could not keep my eyes open. I was going to have to sleep or I wouldn't make it through the next day. I tucked my pistol under my blanket to keep it close, just in case, then drifted off to sleep.

# CHAPTER TEN

When I woke, I heard some movement off to my left. I rolled over and looked. I could see Roth kneeling next to the fire making a pot of coffee. I glanced over my shoulder and saw that Monica was still sound asleep.

I rolled away from her and sat up. After I made sure that no little desert creatures had crawled into my boots during the night, I slipped them on. I walked over and knelt down next to the fire.

"It sure gets cold out here at night," I said quietly.

"It does do that. It can be hotter than hell during the day, then freezing cold at night," he said without looking at me.

"I understand you're with the state police?"

"That's right," he replied as he turned and looked at me.

"Where are you stationed?"

He hesitated, then looked away for a moment as he moved the coffeepot to a different location on the fire. I got the feeling that he was avoiding my question, but why? What possible reason could he have for not wanting to tell me where he was stationed?

"I'm stationed out of the Flagstaff office," he said as he turned back towards me.

He looked at me as if to challenge me. It was almost as if he dared me to ask him another question. I decided that it might be a good idea if I didn't press him for answers, just yet. I figured that I might have better luck asking a question here and a question there. By avoiding asking him a lot of questions all at once, I might get more information out of him without him even realizing it.

"Pretty country up that way," I commented with a smile.

"Yeah, sure is," he replied flatly.

Changing the subject seemed to make him more at ease, but his response still seemed a bit cautious.

"I guess I better get Monica up. I suppose you'd like to get an early start."

"Yeah. It's going to be hot today. We might as well cover as much ground as we can while it's cool."

I nodded that I understood, then stood up. I walked back to where Monica was sleeping and knelt down beside her. I glanced over my shoulder to see if Roth was watching me. At the moment, he was busy fixing breakfast.

"Honey," I said softly as I reached out and touched her on the shoulder.

She turned and looked up at me. A smile came over her face.

"Is it time to get up?"

"Yes. Honey, be sure to keep your gun out of sight."

"Why? What's happening?" she asked as the expression on her face suddenly turned serious.

"I don't know for sure, but I don't like Roth. There's just something about him that doesn't seem to add up. I don't trust him."

Monica nodded that she understood. I sat down on my bedroll. With my back to Roth, I slipped my pistol out from under my bedding, strapped it to my leg, then pulled my pant leg down over it.

I went back over to the fire. I watched as Roth and Roberto prepared breakfast. After everyone had finished eating, we broke camp and started out on the trail again. It took us several hours to get to the cave where Professor Martin had lost his life.

When we arrived, we tied our horses in a clump of small trees. It was like a small island in a sea of rocks. There was grass at the base of the trees that the horses could eat, and a small spring that would provide clear fresh water.

I walked with Monica toward the opening to the cave. While we stood looking at it, Roberto walked up beside us.

"This is where that professor from Minnesota died. He was in the cave when the ceiling collapsed on him," Roberto explained.

"Were you here when it happened?" I asked.

"No. I was with the rescue party. I came to help get his body out."

"You were with the rescue party?" I asked a little confused by his statement.

"Yes."

"Was Roth here, too?"

"Not that I know of. I've never met him before. I've only heard of him."

"Thanks. We're going to take a look around."

"Sure, but I wouldn't go in there, if I was you. I don't think it's very safe," Roberto warned.

"We'll be careful," I assured him.

Roberto shrugged his shoulders, turned and walked back toward the horses while Monica and I walked up closer to the entrance of the cave. I took a few minutes to study the entrance while Monica stood at my side.

"I wonder what they found so interesting about this cave?" I asked more to hear myself think than to really ask a question.

"What do you mean?"

"I was just wondering what made this cave so interesting to Professor Garvey. Remember, Russell Martin said that Garvey insisted that they come to this cave first?"

"Yes, I remember," Monica replied.

"Why did Garvey insist on coming here in the first place?"

"I don't know," Monica replied. "From the looks of it, a lot of people know about this cave and have been here before. Look at all the tracks."

"Say, if you two are going in there, you better take one of these. It goes in quite a ways," Roth called out from the trees.

I turned around and looked at him. He was standing next to one of the packhorses holding up a flashlight. Something about what he said gave me the willies. I got the impression that he wanted us to go into the cave. That didn't set well with me, since Roberto had just advised us not to go in.

Suddenly, I remembered something else Roberto had just told me that didn't set well. He had just finished telling me that he did not know Roth, that he had never seen him before. Yet, Roth had said earlier that he was one of the officers who were here to retrieve Martin's body. From what both of them had told me, they would have had to have been here at the same time. It didn't add up. Someone had to be lying and I was sure that it was Roth.

Needless to say, I was growing rather nervous about Roth. I wondered if we were being set up. It would not surprise me as I was convinced that Jacob Martin had been set up when he was killed in this very cave. There was only one way to find out what was going on, and that was to continue with what we started out to do.

I looked over at Monica. The expression on her face indicated to me that she was as nervous as I was about going into the cave. I don't think she trusted Roth, either. I also knew that it was not likely that we would find any clues as to what happened here unless we did go inside the cave. It was kind of a catch 22, damned if you do, damned if you don't.

"Be right back," I said, then started toward Roth and the packhorses.

"I'd like two of those, if you don't mind," I said as he handed me the flashlight.

He looked at me for a second before he dug into the pack for another flashlight. Maybe I'm paranoid, but he seemed reluctant to give me the second one. While he was looking for a second flashlight, I checked the flashlight I had to make sure that it worked. He finally produced a second flashlight.

"Don't lose them. We don't have any more," he said with a grin.

"I won't," I said as I checked to make sure the second one worked.

As I walked back toward Monica, I could feel Roth watching my back. It was an uncomfortable feeling. It was almost as if he had a gun aimed at the middle of my back and was ready to pull the trigger at any moment. A rather scary feeling, to say the least.

When I got back to where Monica was waiting, I handed her a flashlight. She looked into my eyes. I wasn't sure just what was going on in her head, but I could tell that she was not sure about going into the cave.

"Roth is watching us," Monica whispered as I stepped up beside her.

"Yeah, I know. He seems to be very interested in what we are doing."

She was tense, but then, so was I. At least one person we knew of had already died in the cave. I could not forget what Monica had told me. Sam had said that he heard a bang like a firecracker just before the roof fell in. What was to prevent it from happening again?

If Sam had really heard a bang, then someone would have had to set the charge off from outside the cave. It would have had to go off at just the right moment if it was intended to kill Professor Martin. Someone on the expedition would have had to set off the charge, or someone who knew they were coming here would have to have been waiting nearby.

I knew that Roberto was not on the expedition, but I didn't know about Roth. The way Roth looked at me, the look in his eyes made me jittery. I wasn't sure if he was just not happy with his assignment, which was to take us where we wanted to go, or if he had another reason for his cautiousness.

A thought came to me. I turned around and called out to Roth.

"Hey, Roth. How deep does this cave go?"

"Pretty deep. Maybe five, six hundred feet," he called back.

I waved to let him know that I had heard him, then turned back around. If he knew how deep the cave was, there was no doubt in my mind that he had been in it before. I doubted that he had been here during the rescue. If he had, Roberto would more than likely have seen him. If he wasn't here during the rescue, he would have had to be inside the cave some other time in order to know how deep it went.

I reached out to Monica and took her hand. We started toward the entrance to the cave. As we were just about to enter the cave, Monica pulled on my arm. I stopped and looked at her.

"You better tie your boot before you trip on the laces," she said.

I looked down at my boot. Sure enough, the laces were loose. After handing her my flashlight, I knelt down to tie the laces.

My attention was suddenly drawn away from my boot. I wasn't sure what I was seeing at first. As I tied my boot, I realized that there was a thin wire lying half-hidden in the dirt. I had to wonder what a wire like that was doing here, it seemed out of place.

I glanced back over my shoulder toward the trees where the horses were tied. I saw Roberto sitting on the ground and leaning back against a tree with his hat pulled down over his eyes. He looked like he might be sleeping.

What I didn't see was Roth. He had been there only seconds ago and now he was gone. I immediately wondered where he went. He could have been anywhere.

I finished tying my boot. After a quick look around again, I slipped my pocketknife out of my pocket, reached down alongside my boot and cut the wire. I pushed dirt back over the wire so it could not be seen. I had no idea where it came from, what it might be attached to, or if it was attached to anything at all. But I wasn't about to take any chances.

As I stood up, I looked up at Monica. I could tell by the look on her face that she had seen me cut the wire. She was one smart woman with a cool head. She made no sudden moves and she didn't panic, although I wouldn't have blamed her if she had run like hell.

I reached out and took her arm. I guided her into the cave. Once inside, we stepped back into the darkness, but I didn't turn on my flashlight. Instead, I drew her back away from the entrance, up against the side of the cave.

"Leave your flashlight off."

"What's going on?" she asked.

I could hear the apprehension in her voice, and I certainly could not blame her for that. I had no idea what was going on. I wasn't even sure that what I believed was really the case.

"I think Sam was right. Someone set off a small charge in here that caused the ceiling to collapse."

"What makes you think that?"

"That wire I cut is the same kind of wire that is used to set off dynamite."

Monica's expression did not change but it was clear that she was scared.

"Did you see where Roth went?"

"No."

"When I looked back down the hill, Roberto was sleeping against a tree, but Roth was gone."

"We better get out of here," Monica said, her voice showing how frightened she was.

"Not yet. I want to know what's so important about this cave."

Monica looked at me as if I was crazy, and she might very well have been right. Only a fool would do what I was about to do.

I turned on my flashlight and began shining it around. I started on the ground near the entrance to the cave and worked my way up the walls. When I reached the ceiling, I studied the rock formation. I was looking for weak spots, cracks in the rocks, anything that would indicate the ceiling or walls might be unstable. I found nothing that indicated any weakness in the cave.

"Look for anything that doesn't seem to belong in here, or any cracks in the ceiling that runs more than a couple of feet," I said to Monica as I started to move deeper into the cave.

Again, I started with the ground and worked up the walls to the ceiling. Monica picked up on what I was doing. I was sure that she was nervous about being in the cave, but she began to look, too.

As we slowly worked our way deeper and deeper into the cave, I was beginning to think that we were going to find nothing. I found a lot of footprints in the dirt. The footprints were different sizes and from different kinds of boots.

The more time I spent in the cave the more I began to think that the cave had been nothing more than a trap. Far too many people had been in the cave for it to be of any interest to Sam. If anything had been hidden in the cave hundreds of years ago, it would have been found and removed a long time ago.

"Let's get out of here," I said to Monica.

"Wait," Monica said.

I heard the excitement in her voice. She must have found something as she stood frozen, her flashlight pointed at the wall. I quickly moved over next to her and looked where she was shining her flashlight. There in a thin crack in the wall was a pair of fine wires, the same kind of wires I had cut at the entrance to the cave. I quickly reached into my pocket, took out my pocketknife and cut the wires just in case it was not the same set of wires.

I took a deep breath and looked at Monica. I could see the fear in her eyes.

"Is that what I think it is?" she asked, looking like she was almost afraid to hear my answer.

"Yeah. Let's find out where it goes."

I examined the wire for a moment before I grabbed hold of the ends. I gently pulled on the wires. The end of the wire that was running down the wall ran along the ground. It had been buried in the dirt and ran toward the entrance of the cave.

The wires running up toward the ceiling ran along a deep crack in the wall. I continued to pull on it and followed it deeper into the cave. It ran along a long horizontal crack until it came to a crack that turned up toward the ceiling.

I shined my flashlight up along the crack. There it was. In a small hole carved in the ceiling, I could see the very end of two sticks of dynamite. I could also see the silver color of the blasting cap where the wires were connected to it.

"Look," I said to Monica.

She was standing at my shoulder looking up at the dynamite. She just stood staring at it, not saying a word.

"I think we've seen enough. Come on," I said as I reached out and took hold of her hand.

We started back toward the entrance. Suddenly, she stopped. I turned and looked at her, shining my flashlight so I could see her face.

"Are we just going to leave that dynamite there?"

"Sure. What do you want me to do with it?"

"What if it goes off while someone's in here?"

"It won't go off. We cut the wires."

"But, what if....."

"I don't want to touch it. There may be fingerprints on it. We will come back for it later."

"Are you sure it won't go off?"

"Yes, but if it will make you feel better, I'll go back and pull the blasting cap."

Monica did not answer me, but I could tell by the look on her face that it would make her feel better if I at least removed the blasting cap.

"Wait here," I said.

I squeezed her hand, then went back to where we had found the dynamite. I carefully took hold of the wires and carefully pulled the blasting cap from between the sticks of dynamite, then cut the wires to the cap.

I knew that blasting caps were dangerous so I didn't want to put it in my pocket. A quick look around produced a narrow shelf just above my head. I carefully laid the blasting cap on the rocky ledge. I checked to make sure that it was out of sight and not easy to find. When I was satisfied it was secure, I returned to Monica.

"Feel better now?" I asked.

"Yes," she replied as she took hold of my hand.

"Come on."

We moved rapidly toward the entrance of the cave. When we were getting close, we leaned against the wall and looked out. Roberto was still leaning against the tree, right where he was when we went into the cave. Roth was still nowhere in sight.

"I wonder where Roth is?" Monica mentioned as if reading my mind.

"I don't know," I replied.

I had a feeling that Roth was not far away. It occurred to me that if I followed the wire out of the cave, I would find him at the end of it. If Roth had tried to explode the dynamite, but it hadn't worked because I cut the wire, he would soon be showing his hand.

"I want you to be very careful. Somebody doesn't want us snooping around these mountains, and I think Roth is here to make sure we don't find anything."

"What do you think we should do?"

"For the moment, nothing. I'm going to suggest to Roth that we might want to stay here for a while so we can check out the cave a little closer."

"What will that accomplish?"

"I don't know, but I need time to think."

"But won't it give him more time to find out that the wires have been cut. If he finds that out, he will know we're on to him."

"You have a point, but I think we will have to risk it."

"Look. There's Roth," Monica said. "Take a look at his face."

"Yeah. He looks really disgusted."

"He looks mad as hell," Monica observed.

"I'm sure he is. Let's see what happens when we come out of the cave."

Monica nodded and forced a smile. She took my hand and we stepped out of the cave into the sunlight. We tried to act as if we didn't notice him, but he sure noticed us as we walked down the short slope toward the camp. I could see the look on his face as I turned to look at him. It was easy to see that he had to force himself to smile. The look in his eyes was no smile. He had failed in his mission. There was no doubt in my mind that he would try again at the first opportunity.

"Hi," I called out to Roth.

"Well, did you find anything?" he asked.

The tone of his voice sounded a little sarcastic, but I had the feeling that there was more to it than that. I'm sure he would like to know why the dynamite didn't go off, but to ask us directly would show his hand. I didn't think he was ready for that, yet.

"No," Monica replied. "I would like to go back in again, later. I can't figure out why Professor Garvey showed any interest in this cave."

"What do you mean?" Roth asked.

"The place is full of tracks. Too many people have been in it. Anything that had any value as an artifact or any monetary value would have been removed years ago," she replied.

"Oh?"

"Do you know why Professor Garvey wanted to visit this cave?" Monica asked.

"How would I know? I wasn't with them," Roth replied.

"You know what happened here, I just assumed that you had been part of the expedition."

"You assumed wrong, lady," Roth said sharply.

From the tone of his voice I was sure that Monica had struck a nerve. He seemed a little too defensive to me. I would be interested in knowing where he was at the time the ceiling of the cave fell in, but to ask might prove dangerous.

"I'm sorry," Monica said, then looked at me.

"I would like to look around a little," I said to Monica.

"Okay," Monica agreed, not knowing what I had in mind.

"We'll be back in a little while," I said to Roth as Monica took my hand.

We turned and walked away from the campsite. We turned near the entrance to the cave and walked off along the face of the mountain. We went in the opposite direction that Roth came from just before we came out of the cave.

"Where are we going?" Monica asked in a whisper.

"I would like to know what Roth does once we are out of sight."

As soon as we were out of sight of camp, I pulled Monica back into some heavy brush. I put a finger over my mouth as a sign for her to be quiet. Monica took the hint.

We worked our way back toward the entrance to the cave, staying low and out of sight. It was not long before Roth started toward the entrance to the cave. He kept looking in the direction that we had gone, and then looking down at the ground as he moved closer to the entrance to the cave.

"Looks like he's going inside," Monica whispered.

"Yeah, but did you notice how he looked at the ground? My guess would be that he's looking for a break in the wire."

"What will happen when he finds the blasting cap is missing?"

"I don't know, but I don't plan to wait around to find out."

"What are you going to do?"

"Take him prisoner, if I can."

"What?" she said with surprise.

"It's clear to me that he knows about the dynamite. If he knows about the dynamite, then there's a very good chance that he knows who was involved in killing Martin."

# CHAPTER ELEVEN

We waited in hiding until Roth disappeared into the cave. As soon as we were reasonably sure that he had gone deep enough into the cave that he would not be able to see what was going on outside, I took Monica's hand. We ran down the hill toward the camp where Roberto was sleeping.

As we approached Roberto, I slowed down. I got this strange feeling in my gut. He had been leaning up against that same tree from the time we went into the cave until now without moving so much as an inch. I could not help but think that something was wrong.

"Wait," I said as I stopped and drew Monica close to me.

We both just stood there for a moment or two, looking at him. Even though he had his hat pulled down over his eyes, I was sure that he was dead.

"Wait here," I instructed Monica.

I let go of her hand and stepped up to Roberto. It wasn't until I got close to him that I noticed that his gun was gone. As I reached out and touched his arm, his hand slid off his lap and fell limp at his side. I knelt down beside him, reached out and touched his neck to see if there was a pulse. Before I even touched him I knew what I was going to find, but I had to make sure. He was dead.

I wanted to check him over to find out how he had been killed, but I didn't want to move him. To move him would give away the fact that we knew he was dead.

I turned and looked toward Monica, then stood up and walked back toward her. The expression on her face told me that she already knew what I was going to say.

"He's dead, isn't he?" she asked, her eyes looking up to me.

"Yes. We've got to get out of here."

"What about him? We can't just leave him there."

"We have to. We don't have time to take care of him."

Suddenly, a shot ran out and sand jump up at my feet where the bullet struck the ground. I grabbed Monica's hand and pulled her along behind me as I ran as fast as I could for cover in the thick brush near the spring. Two more shots rang out before we dove headfirst into the underbrush.

I didn't take time to see who was shooting at us or where the shots had come from. Taking cover was my first priority. Besides, we already knew who was shooting at us.

We scrambled along the underbrush on our hands and knees. We crouched down behind a couple of trees to catch our breath. I pulled my pant leg up and retrieved my pistol from my leg holster. I noticed Monica was huddled down at the base of the tree looking at me, her eyes big and glassy.

"It's time to get your gun out, Monica," I said rather sharply.

She looked at me for a moment. The look on her face was that of someone who was confused and frightened, or of someone who didn't know what I was talking about. Suddenly, she seemed to become aware of what was going on, of what was expected of her. She reached inside her blouse and drew out the .25 caliber automatic and readied herself.

"Well Mr.McCord, or should I say Detective Nicholas McCord of the Milwaukee Police Department, it seems that you are a little out of your jurisdiction. Not only that, but you have no back up and have no place to run."

"Maybe, but we have control of the water."

"Just how do you figure that? I have control of all the guns, therefore, I have control of everything."

He sounded just a little too confident to me, but than maybe he had good reason. He may have the firepower, but I was not willing to concede to defeat. To concede to defeat meant to die. I was a long way from giving up to the likes of him and I was a long way from dead.

"Are you so sure?" I said as I looked around for some place that might provide a little better cover.

"Oh, I see. I guess I underestimated you. Maybe I don't have all the firepower, but you couldn't have much. What do you have, a little pop gun hidden in your pant leg?"

I grabbed Monica by the arm and motioned for her to come with me. We moved a little further away from the trees into some heavier brush.

Suddenly, a shot ran out. I could hear the sound of the bullet as it slammed into the tree where we had been. From the size of the chunk of wood that the bullet took out of the tree, and the sound of the shot, it was clear that he had a rifle.

"As you can see, McCord, I have the firepower on my side. It will not take me long to flush you out of there."

There was no doubt in my mind that he was right. He had the larger caliber pistols and at least one rifle, probably more. Since I didn't see any of the other rifles around, there was little doubt in my mind that he had them hidden somewhere.

Not being able to see the entrance to the cave, or any of the surrounding brush, I was having a difficult time trying to figure out exactly where he was hiding. I wasn't sure if he was in the cave, or if he had taken cover in the bushes and rocks near the entrance to the cave, or if he was moving around from one place to another.

If we didn't do something quickly, there was a good chance that he would get us before we could get him. I had to find a place where Monica would be safe while I tried to draw him out where I could get a good shot at him.

A quick look around showed me that there were very few places in this small thicket to hide. I did, however, notice several large boulders where a person could hide just back of the small oasis. It meant running across a narrow clearing.

If Roth was near the cave, he might not be able to see someone run across the clearing. However, if he were in the bushes to the right of the cave, he would have a clear shot at anyone running for cover in the boulders.

There was another problem that I needed to consider. If we took cover in the boulders, he would gain control of the water. I didn't want that to happen. In this heat, it would not take long before we would be in no condition to fight him off. He would be able to win without a fight.

My mind was working at a rate of a mile a minute in an effort to come up with some kind of a solution. I needed to be sure that Monica was safe before I could concentrate on Roth. I again looked over toward the boulders. At the moment, I could see no choice.

"When I give you the signal, I want you to run over there behind those rocks," I said as I pointed to where I wanted her to go.

"What about you?"

"Don't worry about me. I'm going to try to get him to give away his position. Hopefully, I will be able to get him before he gets me."

"And what if you don't?" Monica protested.

"Then you will have to get him. If that happens, let him get close. Don't let him know you have a gun until you're ready to shoot. When he gets close enough to you, empty your gun into him. Shoot for his chest, it's the biggest target," I said calmly and carefully so that there was no doubt about what she needed to do.

I guess I should have put it a little more delicately. From the look on her face, I got the impression she didn't think much of my plan. Monica looked at me as if I had lost it.

I could tell by the look in her eyes that she did not want to leave me. She would rather die with me then leave me. It was a nice thought, but I much preferred not to die at all. If she did what I told her, we stood a fair to middling chance of getting out of this alive.

"Honey, get ready. It's important that you run for cover when I tell you, and run like hell."

I leaned over and kissed her lightly on the cheek. When I tried to let her go, she reached behind my head and pulled me to her. She kissed me hard on the lips, then quickly turned away from me. I didn't want her to leave me, but it was the only chance we had that I could think of. I knew if I waited much longer, I would not be able to send her away.

"Go. Go now," I said sharply.

Without a moment of hesitation, Monica jumped to her feet and began running across the clearing toward the boulders. As soon as she was where Roth might see her, I stood up with my gun pointed toward the cave, waiting and watching for him to show himself.

Suddenly, there he was. He rose up from behind some bushes and put the rifle to his shoulder. I knew that it was going to be a very lucky shot if I even came close to him at this range, but I had to try. I aimed carefully but quickly, and pulled the trigger.

My gun jumped in my hand, and I heard his rifle fire. I fired again. I didn't see where my shots had gone, but I knew I had missed him.

Another shot was fired, but this time it ripped a branch off a bush only inches from my head. I dove for cover and rolled off to the left. I took a quick look back toward the boulders just in time to see Monica disappear behind them.

I let out a sigh of relief. At least Monica was safe for the moment. Now I could concentrate on getting Roth.

As my thoughts turned to Roth, I began to wonder about him. The way Roberto had been killed, silently and quickly, made me think that a professional assassin had killed him. If Roth had killed him, then he was probably not a cop, but a professional killer. If that was the case, then there was a very strong possibility that Roth, the policeman assigned to this trip, was dead. The real Roth's body had probably been dumped in some remote ravine where it was not likely to be found for a very long time, if at all.

The sound of a rifle shot and the sound of a bullet passing through the brush suddenly interrupted my thoughts. It was close, so I knew that he had a pretty good idea where I was. I needed to move.

Looking around, I saw two of the horses standing along the picket line. They were nervous. The gunshots being so close probably made them that way.

I began working my way toward them when another shot was fired. The bullet struck a small tree very close to where I had been. It became clear that he didn't know that I had moved away, but it wouldn't take him long to figure it out.

"I can sit here and shoot all day. I've got the guns and the ammunition. You shouldn't have left your rifle on your horse. Now all you have is a little popgun. I would be willing to guess that all you have is about three, maybe four rounds left in it," he called out with a bit of laughter in his voice.

It was clear that he was confident that he would get me without any difficulty. I wasn't all that sure that he wouldn't, but I had no plans to make it easy for him.

I tried to listen and figure out where he was. When he mentioned the gun and how many shots I had left, I looked at my gun and checked it. I realized that he was right. I had just four bullets left in the gun. That was hardly enough to have any kind of an ongoing shoot-out.

I also realized that he was trying to get me to give away my position. If I responded to him, he would know where I was. I couldn't let that happen.

I found a place where I could see through the brush toward the cave without being seen. I carefully scanned the area, but could not pinpoint him. Even if I could, he was too far away for me to get a good shot at him with the gun I had.

Something moved in the brush near the entrance to the cave. I was sure that it was him, but I could not see him. It was then that I realized that he was working his way around toward the end of the small oasis. If he did that, it would put him closer to Monica and give him a better view of the clearing between the oasis and the boulders.

I crawled on my hands and knees as fast as I could back toward where I had been. Suddenly, a shot ran out that ricocheted off one of the boulders near where Monica was hiding.

I heard Monica let out a scream. It sounded more like a scream from surprise, than what I would have expected to hear if she had been hit. I had no way of knowing for sure if she was hit or not, but she must have realized that I would come to her rescue.

"I'm okay," she yelled to me.

"She may be okay now, but she won't be long," Roth called out with a hint of laughter in his voice. "Once I get rid of you, she's all mine."

It didn't take a genus to figure out what was going on in his mind. As long as I was alive, he would not get close to her.

I worked my way closer to the boulders until I was back where I had started. All I had to do was cross the clearing and I could be with her, but I was sure that it was just what Roth wanted me to do. From where he was now, he would have at least a couple of good shots at me, if I tried to get across the clearing.

I laid down flat on the ground at the base of a small tree. From there I could see him just in case he tried to cross the clearing. It was now a standoff. One of us was going to have to make the first move, but who was willing to risk everything first?

I wasn't sure how long Monica could stand to be in those rocks without water. The sun was hot. There was no breeze to help provide at least a little relief from its rays.

I began to realize that I might have sent her into the rocks to bake in the sun. My plan had failed and now she was at risk. I had hoped to get Roth quickly, but things were not turning out that way. I had to do something and do it quickly.

I looked around the base of the tree toward Roth. I could just barely make out the end of the barrel of his rifle. It was sticking out of a thick bush about three feet above the ground. That indicated to me that he was kneeling behind the bush. If I put a shot into the bush, just below the rifle barrel, I might get real lucky and hit him.

I steadied my gun as best I could and aimed for a spot that I thought might get him. It was going to be a difficult shot at best. He was almost out of range for the gun I was using. If I missed, I would have just three shots left and I would give away my position. I didn't see that I had a choice. I had to take the chance.

I slowly pulled back the trigger as I took careful aim at the spot I had selected on the bush. Suddenly, the gun jumped in my hand with a loud bang. I thought I heard a groan come from behind the bush. I wasn't sure if I had hit him or not. I waited.

Suddenly, there was a flurry of shots. The ground around the base of the tree danced as bullets from a pistol slammed into the dirt.

In my effort to protect myself, I fired another shot toward the bush where I thought the shots were coming from. Suddenly everything went black.

\* \* \*

The next thing I remember was opening my eyes and finding myself looking up at Monica. She was cradling my head in her lap and wiping my face with a wet cloth. The worried look on her face quickly changed to a smile.

"What happened?" I said as I reached up to touch a painful spot on the side of my head.

"Roth shot you. It knocked you out."

"Where is he now?"

"Over there," she said as the smile left her face and she looked over toward the boulders.

My head hurt like hell, but I sat up anyway. I looked toward the boulders, but didn't see Roth. I turned back in time to see the look on Monica's face. She was still worried about me, but it was more than that.

"You should take it easy," she suggested.

"You want to explain what happened?"

I got the impression that she didn't really want to talk about it. She looked down at me and let out a sigh.

"When I saw you were shot I wanted to come to you, but I saw Roth come out of the bushes. He had a gun in his hand and was holding his arm. I knew that you had shot him, but I didn't think he was hurt very bad. I think he thought you were dead.

"When he looked up toward me, I knew he would be coming after me. I retreated back in between a couple of large boulders and waited. When he came into sight again, he was only about ten feet from me.

"I remembered what you told me to do. I aimed my gun at him and pulled the trigger. I pulled it again and again until it was empty," she said, her voice choking as she described her encounter with Roth.

"He looked very surprised at first, but then he closed his eyes and fell at my feet. I wasn't sure if he was dead, but he wasn't moving. I crawled around him and I ran down here to you. I was afraid that you were dead."

"I'm not, but my head sure as hell hurts," I said as I reached out and drew her close to me.

I held her in my arms, her head on my shoulder. I was so happy that she was all right that I almost forgot about the pain in my head.

After we held onto each other for several minutes, I leaned away from her. She looked at me. She seemed to know that it was time to get ourselves organized.

"We better get Roberto covered up," I suggested.

"What about Roth?"

"I'll check on him in a minute."

As I stood up, I felt a little dizzy. After a couple of deep breaths, the dizziness sort of went away. We walked back to the camp. She had her arm around me, and I rested my arm over her shoulder.

I left Monica at the fire pit while I got Roberto's sleeping bag. After laying it beside Roberto, I rolled him over on it and wrapped him up in it. Once it was zipped up, I tied the end closed then dragged him into the cave.

When I returned, Monica had built a fire and had coffee going. I sat down on a rock to catch my breath.

"He should be all right in the cave. At least he won't be out in the hot sun," I said as I took a breather.

"What about Roth?" Monica asked.

"I got a feeling that his name isn't Roth."

"Who do you think he is?"

"I don't know, but I'm going to find out," I said as I stood up.

"Maybe you should rest a little longer first. You took a nasty bump on the head."

"I'll rest as soon as I get Roth in the cave."

I got up and grabbed Roth's sleeping bag. Monica stayed at the campsite while I went into the rocks to find Roth. I found him lying face down in the sand between two large boulders, right where Monica said he would be.

I bent down and touched his neck to see if he was dead. He was as dead as they come. After taking his gun, I rolled him over. There on the ground were six spent casings from Monica's .25 caliber automatic, and six neat, well-placed holes in the center of Roth's chest.

I took his holster off him and strapped it around my waist. After putting his gun in the holster, I dragged him out from between the rocks. I took his wallet from his hip pocket, then put him in his sleeping bag and tied the end closed. Hoisting him up over my shoulder, I carried him to the cave.

When I returned to the camp, I found myself exhausted. I needed to rest. Between the excitement, being shot at, and getting shot in the head, I was worn out.

"You should rest," Monica suggested.

"You don't have to tell me that twice."

I dropped down on the sleeping bag, rolled onto my back and closed my eyes. Monica knelt down above my head and began to gently rub my temples. It wasn't long and the pain had subsided and I was feeling very relaxed. The last thing I remember was Monica kissing me lightly on the forehead.

# CHAPTER TWELVE

I was only half-awake but I could hear something that sounded like the scraping of a pan. It sounded as if it was far away at first, but seemed to be getting closer as I became aware of my surroundings. I could also smell something that called me to open my eyes, but my eyes did not want to open.

When I finally did open my eyes, I realized that the sun was setting. The shadows were long and the jagged rocky face of the mountain was a silvery gray and reached up to a darkening sky.

I turned and looked in the direction that the sound seemed to be coming from. There was Monica kneeling beside the fire. She was stirring something in a frying pan over the fire.

I laid quietly and watched her for a minute. This woman never ceased to amaze me. She was beautiful, sexy, talented, and intelligent. She also looked as much at home cooking over an open fire in the middle of nowhere as she did in a modern kitchen.

Just then she turned and looked at me. A broad smile came over her face.

"How are you feeling?" she asked.

"Much better, I think," I said, my head still hurting a little.

"Are you hungry?"

"Yes," I replied as I sat up.

"Good. Dinner should be ready shortly."

"I think I'll go wash my face."

Monica watched me as I stood up slowly. As I walked passed her, she reached up and took hold of my hand. I stopped and looked down into those cobalt blue eyes.

"I love you," she whispered looking up at me.

"I love you, too," I replied, then let go of her hand.

I walked on to the sink size pool where the spring came out of the ground. I knelt down and splashed the cool water on my face and ran my wet hands through my hair.

The cool water felt good. I took a drink, then sat back on my heels to look out over the desert below. The setting sun filled the sky with an array of colors, from bright yellows, to deep oranges, to beautiful purples.

To the west, I could see a number of clouds that caused the colors to mix and blend into a spectacular scene. It seemed strange that there could be such a beautiful and peaceful sunset after a day that had been filled with violence and death.

Two people were dead. One of them just because he was here. The other because he tried to kill us and failed. What was going on here? Who was this man we had called Roth?

It was then I remembered that I had taken his wallet before wrapping him up in his sleeping bag. His wallet might not only tell us who he really was, but might just help us find out who had hired him.

I returned to the camp and found Monica dishing up the dinner she had prepared. The smile quickly faded from her face when I walked right by her and returned to the sleeping bag where I had been resting.

"What happened to Roth's wallet," I said as I searched the sleeping bag.

"Here it is," I said as I found it buried in one of the folds of the bag.

"Can't that wait until after dinner?"

I turned to look at her and saw the look on her face. I was sure that she had worked hard to prepare our dinner.

After giving it a second or two of thought, I could see no reason that searching Roth's wallet couldn't wait. After all, we were not going anywhere, not tonight.

"Sure," I said as I dropped the wallet back on the sleeping bag.

I moved over by the fire and sat down on the rock beside Monica. She handed me a plate. It was heaped high with some kind of a stew.

"I'm sorry, honey," I apologized.

"That's okay," she replied.

I looked at the dish. I wasn't sure what it was that I was about to eat, but it looked good, and it smelled good. I took my fork and speared a piece of the meat. After I put it in my mouth, I began chewing on it. It was tender and very tasty.

"This is good. What is it?"

"I think its called beef stew," she said with a grin.

I looked at her for a minute, not really sure if she was kidding me or not. I looked at the plate, then back at her. There was a sparkle in her eyes.

"It's beef stew, silly. I opened a couple of cans and heated it over the fire."

I looked at the stew again, then back at her. I started to laugh. I had assumed that she had spent all afternoon fixing it.

"Stew? Beef stew?"

"Yes."

"Well I don't care if it is out of a can or not, it tastes good."

We had a good laugh, then settled down to eat. The stew was good, very good. I wasn't sure if it was because we had been out in the fresh air all day, or if it was just because I was hungry. Since it really didn't matter, I ate my fill.

After we finished eating, we cleaned up our dishes and put them away. As soon as we finished getting our campsite back in order, Monica sat back down on the rock next to the fire. I retrieved the wallet from my sleeping bag and joined her on the rock.

The sun had set and a full moon was slowly coming up over the top of the mountain. With the light of the fire and a flashlight, I began going through Roth's wallet. The first thing was the driver license. It was in the name of Michael Morris.

"Well, I guess that answers one of our questions," Monica said.

"At least we know that he isn't Bill Roth. But that brings up another question. Where's Bill Roth?"

Monica looked at me. From the look on her face, I was sure that she was thinking the same thing I was. If the body I had put in the cave was not Bill Roth, then what happened to Roth? Assuming that Roth was to meet up with us and Morris took his place, it was fair to assume that Roth was dead and his body was laying out in the desert somewhere. If that was the case, then who was Michael Morris?

"Anything else in the wallet?" Monica asked as she looked back at it.

"A few credit cards, all in the name of Michael Morris. There are a couple of pictures of a young woman, a picture of a dog, and several pieces of paper with numbers on them. They look like phone numbers. I don't see any names to go with the phone numbers," I said as I examined the slips of paper.

"Not much to go on, is it?" Monica said with a sigh of discouragement.

"I agree that there's not much help here, but after we get back to town we will have the phone numbers and the credit cards checked. They might just help us find out who is behind all this."

"You're right. There may be more here than I thought."

"If we can find out who this guy really is, we might be able to find out who hired him to dispose of us."

"Do you think Michael Morris might be an assumed name, too?"

"Could be," I replied, not being sure of anything at this point.

"Do you think these numbers might help us find out who killed Sam?"

"They might, once we find out who the numbers belong to. If we go on the assumption that Martin was killed to stop the first expedition, and carry that assumption to include that his death is in some way connected to Sam's death, then we might be able to find out who is responsible for all the deaths."

"I find it difficult to believe that Sam would spend more than just a few minutes here. It would not have taken him more than a few minutes to figure out that this cave held nothing of interest to him," Monica said.

"That's just it. I don't believe that Sam ever went into the cave. Martin was killed while seeing if the cave was safe, remember?"

"Yes," Monica replied.

"I'm convinced that Roth, or should I say Morris, killed Martin before Sam had a chance to look in the cave. The death of Martin ended the expedition before it really got under way. I think Morris was trying to kill us the same way he killed Martin, and for the same reason."

"But what is the reason?" Monica asked.

"The reason being to keep us from going any further. I have just two questions. What is it that we might find if we continue, and who's trying to keep us from going on?"

"I doubt we are going to find who was trying to keep us from going on while we are still here. We will need to return to town," Monica said.

"You might be right, but I don't think we should be so quick to return to town," I said as I looked around our campsite.

"Why not? We don't have a guide, and we don't know this country," Monica said as she looked at me.

"You're right on both counts. We don't have a guide, but we have the photos as a guide to where Sam had been. We also have the geological maps and a compass, the first and still one of the best GPS systems ever invented, to keep us from getting too lost," I explained as I tried to get her to be open-minded about what we should do next.

"We do have plenty of supplies," Monica said after giving it some thought.

"If we watch our supplies, keep plenty of water and take our time. We might be able to find what Sam was looking for before anyone realizes that Morris failed to get rid of us," I reminded her. "Besides, we still need to find out what it was that Sam was looking for if we are to find out why he was killed,"

"Okay," she replied thoughtfully. "I agree that we have a head start if we continue, but do we have enough of a head start?"

"I figure we have two, maybe three days head start before anyone figures out that Morris failed to kill us. You game to go on?" I asked.

"Yes," she replied with a smile. "I'm game. I can't think of anyone else I would rather be lost in the desert with than you."

"Gee, thanks. I'm so glad that you have confidence in me," I replied as I leaned over and kissed her.

"So, what do we do now?" she asked with a grin.

"We'll spend the night here and leave first thing in the morning. I think we should head north," I suggested.

"Sounds good to me. I don't know about you, but I would sleep better if I had a bath," Monica said.

"A bath? How are you going to get a bath out here? That spring is only about the size of a bathroom sink."

"I take it that you don't know that there's a small pool about the size of a large bathtub just fifty to sixty feet down the hill from the spring?"

"No, I didn't."

"I found it while you were resting. It's fed by the spring and is hidden in the bushes."

"Oh, really," I replied with a smile.

"There's a full moon tonight," she informed me in that sexy voice of hers.

"Yes, I know. Might I suggest that we take a nice long bath and then get a good night's sleep? It might be awhile before we get a chance to enjoy either again," I suggested.

"I take it you mean for us to take a bath together?" she asked playfully with a sparkle in her eyes and a grin on her face.

"Yes. That is what you had in mind in the first place, isn't it?"

"Well, yes. But I kind of wanted it to be your idea," she said as she reached over and put her hand on my knee.

I stood up and reached out a hand to her. She stood up and together we walked down the hill to the small pool.

The small pool was fed from one end by a narrow stream that flowed down from the spring. The water then flowed out the other end of the pool and on down the hill. The flow of the water kept the water in the pool clean and clear.

Standing in the moonlight, next to the pool, I took Monica in my arms. She tipped her head back and looked up at me, a soft smile on her face. I leaned down until our lips met.

It was a long passionate kiss. It was the kind of kiss that is intended to reach to the deepest recesses of a person's being. Every nerve in my body was aware of the beautiful woman in my arms. I could not have planned a better night if I had tried.

I let go of her and stepped back. In the glow of the moonlight, we watched each other as we undressed. When we were naked, we stood and looked at each other for a moment. Monica's beautiful body glowed in the light of the moon. I could not remember a time in my life when I had seen anyone so lovely.

Monica stepped up to me and put her hands on my chest. As I reached out, I put my hands on her narrow waist and drew her to me. I then wrapped my arms around her. The feel of her body pressing against me raised my desire for her.

"A bath," she reminded me in a soft whisper as she looked up at me.

"A bath," I conceded.

I took my arms from around her and took hold of her hand. Together we waded into the small pool. After I sat down in the shallow water, she sat down beside me. She rolled over against me as I wrapped her in my arms.

We lay naked in the cool spring water. We let the cool water rinse away the dust and the sweat from our bodies. The feel of her warm body contrasted against the coolness of the water allowed me to forget the events of the day. Even my headache was gone.

After spending a while just letting the cool water rinse away the sweat, Monica stood up and walked out of the pool.

"I'll be right back," she said as walked away from me.

The droplets of water on her naked body sparkled in the glow of the moonlight as she walked back toward our camp. Her movements were smooth and graceful. It was a pleasure just to watch her move.

Within a few minutes she returned with a bar of soap and a grin on her face.

"You first," she said as she stepped back into the pool and held the bar of soap out to me.

There was no doubt in my mind what she wanted me to do. I first washed her back and then she washed mine. After we finished washing each other, we rinsed off the soap. We then curled up in each other's arms in the clear water of the pool and under the glow of the moonlight.

After we made love, we returned to our sleeping bags where we spent the rest of the night wrapped in each other's arms. We slept curled up together until the dawn.

* * *

As I began to wake and reality returned to the recesses of my mind, I could hear the sounds of some kind of bird as it sang in the trees. As my senses seemed to clear, I could feel something warm against my side and on my chest. Even before I opened my eyes, I knew that it was Monica.

I opened my eyes and looked toward her. She was lying on her side up against me, one hand resting on my chest. She had her head resting on her other hand as she looked down at me.

"How long have you been watching me sleep?" I asked.

"Not long," she replied in a whisper.

"Come here," I whispered.

As she leaned down over me, she slid her hand off my chest and on up to my shoulder. I reached out and held her to me as we kissed.

It was a long passionate kiss. I could feel the warmth of her bare breasts pressing against my chest, and her leg curled up over mine. I did not want this moment to end.

She rose up and looked down at me. I knew that no matter how much I wanted to stay here, we had things that had to be done.

"You ready to get up and get dressed?" she asked.

"No. I would rather stay right here, just like we are."

"But I don't have a thing on."

"I know," I replied with a devilish grin. "Admit it, you would like to stay here, too."

"Yes. Yes I would," she admitted with a grin. "I would like to spend the whole day lying here with you and taking baths in the pool."

"But we can't, can we? We have a lot to do," I said.

Monica didn't answer me. She already knew what the answer was, just as I did.

Reluctantly, Monica rolled off me and onto her back. I sat up and looked over my shoulder at her. I would have given anything to spend the whole day with her, right here.

Monica let out a sigh, then sat up. The light blanket that had covered her fell down to her waist. I found it difficult to take my eyes off her. If I were going to get us moving, I would have to get started.

"I'll be right back," I said as I stood up.

As I walked toward the spring to wash my face, I was sure that I could feel her watching me. I guess it was only fair; after all, I liked to watch her.

After I washed my face, I walked down to the pool. There on the ground, right where we had left them, were our clothes. I gathered them up and carried them back to our camp.

When I got there, Monica was already dressed and was building a fire to prepare breakfast. She glanced over at me and smiled. I wasn't sure if the smile was because I was still not dressed, or if the handful of clothes reminded her of last night at the pool.

"I thought we better have a good breakfast before we start out," she said.

"Good idea," I replied as I slipped into my jeans.

While Monica prepared breakfast, I saddled the horses and put the packs on the packhorses. I wasn't sure just what to do with the two extra horses we had now. If we took them with us it would mean that we would need to carry that much more water. But on the other hand, we had the extra horses to carry the extra water.

I checked the supplies and found that we didn't have any extra containers to carry extra water in. After giving it a bit of consideration, I decided that I would turn the two extra horses loose. With plenty of food and water right here, they were not likely to go very far. We could return for them later.

As soon as I had the horses ready, I returned to the camp. All that was left to do was to eat and pack up what few items we were still using. I found Monica dishing up a couple of large omelets.

"I hope you're hungry," she said as she handed me a plate.

"I am. These people really know how to pack," I said as I took the plate.

"I doubt that we will be eating this well for a while. It seems that the rest of the food is canned or freeze dried."

I sat down on the rock near the fire. After setting a couple of cups of coffee on the rock next to me, Monica joined me.

We didn't talk very much. We were both deep in thought and busy eating. I think we both knew that from now on the trip was going to be hard. If we failed to find what we were looking for, we would leave many questions unanswered. We also knew that with what little we had to go on, we might never find out where Sam had been killed, or why. If we didn't find out where Sam was murdered and why, it would forever be just speculation.

As soon as we finished eating, we cleaned up the area and doused the fire with water. It was now time to figure out which way we were going.

"You want to get the copies of the photographs we took from Sam's office? I'll get the maps," I asked.

Monica nodded, then went to her pack for the copies. I got the geological maps and spread them out on a large flat rock. When she returned, she spread the copies we had taken from Sam's office out on the rock next to the map. We studied the copies carefully. We had to have the first one right or we could end up going in the wrong direction.

I looked from the copies to the mountain, then back to the copies. Nothing seemed to fit. None of the copies gave us the answers we needed.

"Nick?"

"Yeah?"

"I think we need to go north, toward the northern part of the mountains," Monica said.

"What makes you think we should go that way?"

"I don't know. Maybe it was something you said awhile back, I just don't know."

"That's as good a reason as I can come up with. That area seems to be rugged. It's more so than some of the other areas. The areas in these copies look rugged. I think it would be a good idea if we go that way. Going south would only take us back the way we came."

"I have another suggestion," Monica said.

"What? I'm open to any suggestions at this point."

"Maybe if we split up the copies of the photos so we only have to concentrate on three at a time instead of all six, we might stand a better chance of recognizing the rock formations when we see them. What do you think?"

"I think that's a good idea. Why don't you take these and I'll take these." I said as I divided up the photos. "If you think you see a formation that looks like one of the pictures, we'll stop and compare notes,"

After I gave Monica three of the copies of the photos and I took the other three, I folded up the geological map and put it in my shirt pocket along with the compass. We walked over to the horses. I slipped a rifle into each scabbard of the saddles.

While Monica mounted up, I untied the two horses that we were going to leave behind. They were completely free to go anywhere they wanted, but they seemed content to stay where there was plenty of water and grass.

I mounted up and grabbed the lead to the packhorses. I motioned for Monica to lead the way. She started out at a slow walk. I noticed that she started looking for some sign that we were headed in the right direction even before we had left the campsite.

I glanced back over my shoulder. The two horses didn't seem to care that we were leaving them behind. Why should they? They had everything they needed, and they didn't have to do any of the work.

As soon as the camp was out of sight, I began to scan the rocky formations for something that would come close to matching the copies of the photos I had. I was sure that we could go on for miles before we might see something. Then there was always the possibility that we could go on for days and see nothing. We didn't even know if we were headed in the right direction.

# CHAPTER THIRTEEN

The minutes stretched into hours. The long narrow trail seemed to be getting steeper and steeper, as well as narrower. I was beginning to think that every rock formation in these mountains looked the same.

As I gazed at a rocky ridge off to my left, I remembered something that Morris had said early yesterday morning. He had said something to the effect that we would not be able to take the horses all the way. I wasn't sure what he meant by that, but if he had been right there was a good chance that we were on the right trail.

We had only traveled a fairly short distance when we found the first place in our photo map. It required us to take a turn onto another trail that seemed to go deeper into the mountains. Over the next few hours or so we found a couple more of the formations in the photos. It seemed to me that they had gotten progressively harder to find.

We had traveled what I felt was a long ways from the last formation without seeing anything that I thought would be helpful in getting to our goal when we suddenly came upon a deep, wide cut in the ground. It was at least forty to forty-five feet wide and probably fifteen to twenty feet deep. The cut ran back toward the face of the mountain. It was obvious that water rushing down through the canyon during spring rains had caused flash floods that washed out part of the trail. It was a pretty steep drop into the wash.

"What do you think?" Monica asked as she turned in the saddle and looked back over her shoulder at me.

"I don't know. It looks like our trail has been cut-in two. Do you think you can get your horse down into the wash without getting hurt?"

Monica got off her horse and walked to the edge. As she looked into the wash, I noticed that she not only looked down and across the wash, but she looked up and down it. I suspected that she was checking it out in the hope of seeing an easier place to cross.

"This looks like the best place to cross. I think we can make it," she said as she turned toward me. "It's pretty steep, but I think the horses can make it."

"Unless you have a better idea, I say we press on."

Monica nodded her agreement then got back in the saddle. She coaxed the animal over the edge. The horse was reluctant to take the first step, but finally gave in and slid over the edge. Monica disappeared from sight for a few seconds. I felt a strong sense of relief when she appeared in the bottom of the wash, safe and intact.

I knew I was not as good on a horse as she was, but it was my turn. If I hung onto the saddle tightly, I would probably make it okay. The horse didn't want to slide down the embankment any more than Monica's horse had, but he went over the edge as soon as he saw Monica's horse waiting below. Luckily the packhorses followed without any problems. They seemed to accept it all in stride. It was just another day in the life of a packhorse. I had to wonder if they had been here before.

Once we were in the bottom of the draw, Monica got off her horse and looked around. I wasn't sure if there was anything wrong or not, or if she just needed to get out of the saddle for a few minutes. The look on her face indicated that there might be some sort of problem. I got off my horse and walked over to her.

"What's the matter?"

"Have you looked around?" she asked.

"No, not really," I replied, but took the hint.

I slowly looked at each side of the draw, and up and down the wash. It didn't take a genius to figure out that we might have gotten down in the draw without much trouble, but getting out of it was going to be a different matter. The sides were steep and didn't look as if they were solid enough for the horses to get good footing to get back up to the top.

"I see what you mean," I said as I turned back toward her.

Monica had turned around. She had her back to me and was looking up the draw toward the mountain. I wondered what she was looking at. Whatever it was, she seemed almost hypnotize by it.

"What is it?" I asked as I stepped up beside her.

"This is it," she said in a soft whisper, her eyes sparkling with excitement.

"What is it?"

"This is where we go," she said as she pointed up the draw.

"You mean up this canyon?"

"Yes."

"Are you sure?"

"Yes. This is the way we have to go."

Needless to say, I was a little worried about going up the canyon. It was clear that it had been washed out only a few days ago. If a sudden rain should come, we could get caught in a flash flood and have no place to go. From what I could see, there was nothing but steep rocky walls on both sides, in some places they were going up over a hundred feet or more.

"Well, if you say so, let's go."

"Nick?"

"Yeah?"

"I'm sure this is where one of the pictures was taken from. The shadows are a little different, but I think the rock formations are the same. The photo must have been taken either earlier or later in the day."

"I believe you," I said in an effort to reassure her.

"I know it is."

"Would you feel better if I look at the picture?"

"Yes," she admitted.

Monica took the copies of the photos out of her pocket. After quickly going through them, she handed me the one that she thought showed the draw. I looked back and forth from the photocopy to the canyon and back to the photocopy again several times. The shadows were a little longer and it looked like the picture might have been taken from a slightly different angle, but I was sure she was right.

I took a look up at the sky. There were only a few fluffy clouds. Nothing to indicate that it would rain soon, but it really didn't matter. We were in the draw with apparently no easy way out. Since we were already here, we might as well go on. We might even find a way out.

"I'd like to get moving while we still have some light. Once the sun goes down, these canyons can get pretty dark very quickly," I said as I looked up the canyon.

"I agree. We don't know where this will lead us."

We mounted up. I motioned for Monica to lead the way. As her horse started picking its way around the rocks and boulders on the canyon floor, I followed along with the packhorses.

The draw was fairly steep and very rocky, and quickly turned into a deep canyon. The ground was loose and the footing for the horses was unstable. It was slow going. If it got much rougher, we would have to find a place to leave the horses.

I continued to look around as we moved further up the canyon. In the course of looking for a way out of the canyon that we might use on our return, I noticed that we had passed by several high rocky peaks. I was sure that meant that we had move from one side of the ridge to the other.

I kept my eyes open and moving. Suddenly, I realized that I was looking at one of the rock formations that I had a picture of. Monica had already gone past it.

"Monica, wait."

She stopped and turned in the saddle. Looking back over her shoulder, she saw me pointing to a narrow trail that went up the side to the cliff. It would make a good place for us to get out of the canyon, but was it the right place?

After she looked at it for a minute or two, she turned and rode back to me.

"Is this where we're supposed to go?" she asked as she looked up at the narrow trail.

"I don't know, but it looks exactly like the picture."

I held out the picture and gave her a chance to look at it. As she studied it, I noticed that her head was bobbing slightly in agreement.

"Do you suppose this is the place where Morris knew that we would have to leave the horses?" Monica asked.

"I don't know, could be," I replied as I looked around. "If it is, I don't have the foggiest idea where we're supposed to leave them. If we leave them here, there is nothing for them to eat or drink."

"How about one of us going up along the trail for a little ways. Never know what we might see from up there," she suggested.

"Good idea. I'll go up and around that bend at the top. I can check it out from there," I said as I pointed to the place where the trail turned and disappeared. "You wait here with the horses."

"Please be careful."

"I will," I said as I climbed down from the saddle.

Monica climbed down, too. I handed her the reins to my horse. After a quick look around, I pulled my rifle out of the scabbard. I noticed the look on Monica's face.

"Just in case, honey."

Monica smiled, indicating that she understood. I had no intentions of making the same mistake I had made back at the cave. I was not about to get caught without some heavy firepower again.

I turned and walked toward the narrow trail. It was fairly steep, but not that difficult a walk as long as I watched my step. The surface of the trail was made up of decomposing granite. It had a tendency to cause a person to slip. It was like walking on marbles. I was sure that the horses would be able to get up it, if we walked them and took our time.

Within a few minutes I found myself looking down into the canyon. Monica was standing next to the horses looking up at me. Even from this height, I could see the worried look on her face.

When I finally reached the place where the trail was going to turn a bend and I would be out of Monica's sight, I took a second to look down at her again. This time, she was too far away for me to see her very well.

I also took a minute to look around. Off to the west I could see the flat desert spread out for miles. To the northwest, I could see rough rocky hills and even a few pillars of rock sticking up above the otherwise rock and cactus covered ground. To the south, I could see nothing but the rocky surface of the mountains. It looked beautiful, yet barren.

In front of me was a narrow trail that showed no signs that it had been used in years. From the few western books that I had read over the years, I got the feeling that it might have been an old Indian trail, one that had not been used for centuries.

I wasn't sure why I felt that way. It could have been just my imagination running wild and working overtime. After all, I was in the Superstition Mountains, a place full of legends and mysteries.

My thoughts returned to remind me why I was here. I took one last look down at Monica. I waved and watched as she waved back.

As I turned away, I started around the bend. It was an up hill climb. I suddenly found myself on a plateau. It looked very flat, rocky and void of any kind of plant life. I could see nothing that would help us in our quest.

I also knew that not everything was as it seemed. Places that appeared to be flat often had ravines and gullies crossing them. Places that seemed void of life, often had more life than one would think.

After walking out onto the plateau a little way, I soon discovered that the small plateau held little of interest to us. I was convinced that it was as flat as it appeared. I turned around and started back toward the canyon where I had left Monica. So far, I had seen nothing except for rocky cliffs that rose up from the flat surface of the plateau on two sides, and what looked like shear drop-offs on the other sides.

As I started to slowly move back to the narrow trail, I looked off across the deep canyon where I had left Monica. Something caught my eye. I stopped to take a better look. It was then that I noticed that there appeared to be some areas on the plateau that looked green. If what I thought I was seeing was correct, there was a good chance that there was some kind of plant life over there. And plant life meant there was water.

I scanned the area as best I could and discovered what looked like a narrow crack in the surface of the flat plateau on the other side of the canyon. From where I was, just a little above it, it looked like nothing more than a narrow scar in the ground, but I knew that at this distance that crack could very well be three or four feet wide, maybe more. I also noticed that it wandered around and came to an end near the steep bank of the canyon wall not more than a few yards behind Monica.

My first thought was how could we get over there. I began to wonder if that deep crevice in the rock might provide a way to get to the top of the plateau. If it was a way up to the top, it might prove to be a good place to leave the horses. Where there was plant life, there had to be water.

I stopped again at the edge of the canyon, before I started back down. I needed to find out where the crack in the plateau came out into the canyon.

I must have captured Monica's attention by stopping and looking across the canyon. She was calling out to me, but I could not hear what she was saying. I waved down to let her know that everything was okay. I took a little longer to get a good look at the deep grooves in the canyon wall, so that when I got to the bottom of the canyon, I would have a good idea where it came out.

I hurried as best I could back to where Monica was waiting. When I arrived in the bottom of the canyon and looked across to where the furrow in the rock should have appeared in the wall of the cliff, I could see nothing. I couldn't believe that it had simply disappeared. It had to be there, I could see it from up on the trail.

"Look over there," I said to Monica. "Do you see a break, or an opening in that rock formation anywhere?"

I waited until Monica looked toward where I was pointing. She seemed to be looking with the hope of seeing what I saw, but she could not see anything, either.

"No," she said as she turned and looked at me.

"I can't see it either, but there is an opening right there. I think it's big enough to get a horse through."

"Are you sure," she asked as she looked again. "I don't see anything."

"I can't see it from here, but I could see it from up above. It looks like it could be a trail that leads up to the top. There are some plants up there. That means there's water."

"What about up there?" she asked as she pointed back to where I had been.

"There's nothing up there but rocks and shear cliffs. But I saw something green, in fact a good deal of green on this side," I replied as I took the reins of my horse and started across the canyon floor toward where I thought the opening should be.

Monica followed me as if she believed me. I don't know why. I wasn't even sure that I believed there was a deep, wide break in the steep, rocky wall myself.

It wasn't until I could almost reach out and touch the rock wall that I could see the entrance to what looked like a very narrow canyon. I stepped up to the entrance and looked into the canyon. For almost fifteen feet it sort of ran back in behind the rock wall, almost parallel to the face of the cliff, then turned slightly. The color of the rock and the horizontal cracks and fissures hid the entrance to the canyon so well that even standing in front of it, it was difficult to see.

"Look here," I said as I stood in the entrance to the narrow canyon.

Monica looked, but I could see by the expression on her face that she was not sure about it. It was narrow with shear walls on both sides that went almost straight up. It was so narrow that if we got several yards into the canyon, we would not be able to turn the horses around to get back out.

"This could be a dead end. If we get back in there and it doesn't go anywhere, it would be hard to get back out," she said as she looked into the narrow canyon.

I had no problem agreeing with her assessment of the situation, but I couldn't help believing that this was the direction that we were to take.

"I think Sam wanted us to go up that trail on the other side. He knew that we would not see the entrance from down here, but we might see it from up on top. You could look right at the entrance and not even see it if you didn't know it was here. The only way to know it was here was to see it from the top of the other side of the wash."

"You might be right," Monica said after giving it some thought.

"What do you say? Do we follow it?" I asked.

I could see that Monica was mulling it over in her mind. I couldn't blame her for being cautious. It was the perfect place for a trap. Once inside, there was no turning back.

"Okay," she said as she straightened her shoulders.

Monica was one determined lady. She was willing, and once she set her mind to something, she was ready to do it. We were ready.

"Nick?"

"Yeah?"

"Do you think we should make sure that we are not leaving a trail someone could follow?"

It was a good question. I had not thought that there would be anyone following us, after all, I hadn't figured on anyone starting to miss us for at least a couple of days.

The more I thought about it, the more sense it made. If someone was going to all the trouble of keeping us from getting up here, they were bound to have an alternative plan just in case Morris failed to stop us at the cave.

"You have a good point. We'll take the horses into the canyon, then I'll come back and make sure we didn't leave a trail."

I tied the reins of the first packhorse to my saddle, then tied the second packhorse to the first. This way they could walk single file through the canyon. As soon as we were ready, I took the reins of my horse and led him into the narrow canyon. The other horses followed along without a problem. Monica followed behind, leading her horse.

After we had gone about two hundred feet up the canyon, I stopped. I wanted to tie my horse so that he would stay put, but there was nothing but rock cliffs on either side. I decided that there was only one way for him to go and that was on up the canyon. It was too narrow for him to turn around.

I dropped the reins on the ground and pushed my horse over against one side of the canyon. I was able to squeeze by him, but not without some difficulty. It was a little more difficult for me to get past the packhorses, but I managed by getting down on my hands and knees so I could pass under the packs.

I took a minute to get a kiss from Monica before I squeezed past her horse. Once I was past her horse, I walked to the entrance of the canyon. I took a minute to look around before stepping out in the open.

Monica's reminder of the possibility that we might be followed had alerted me to many of the dangers that could still befall us. We were not only trying to find the treasure that Sam had been looking for, we were trying to stay alive long enough to find out who had killed him. We were also trying to avoid any others that were involved in the effort to prevent him or us from finding what Sam was looking for.

As soon as I was sure that it was clear, I began checking the ground for signs that we had passed this way. I had to laugh at myself as I thought about what I was doing. I was a city boy. What did I know about tracking? I could remember reading somewhere that even on rocky ground a horse will leave scratches on rocks. Some real good trackers would be able to follow such a trail.

I looked around, examining the rocks where we had been. I found a couple rocks that had scratches on them. I couldn't be sure if they were from the horse's shoes, or something else. Just to be on the safe side, I turned the rocks over to cover the marks on them. It may not have been the thing to do, but it was all I could think of. At least if we were being tracked, I would not be making it easy to be followed.

Once I was reasonably satisfied that we had not left a trail that could be easily followed, I returned to the canyon. Once again I squeezed past the horses until I was in front of my horse. I picked up the reins and began the trek up the narrow canyon.

It was slow going as the trail was covered with loose granite that had a tendency to roll under our feet, plus it was steep. In several areas we came across some fairly large rocks that proved to be difficult to get around. Several places were so narrow that the packs on the packhorses rubbed against both sides of the canyon walls at the same time. It also wound around, often making it impossible for me to see Monica and her horse behind us.

It took several hours to wind our way up the dark shadowy canyon, but suddenly we broke out into the sunlight on top of the plateau. I was surprised by the size of the plateau. It must have been close to four, maybe five hundred acres, and it was not as flat as it appeared.

We quickly discovered that it was crisscrossed with very shallow ditches that looked like small channels, trenches and troughs. The trenches were filled with lush green grass and there were even a few small pockets of water.

It quickly became apparent to me that I had seen only a small part of the plateau from the other side of the wash. It was also clear that the plateau could easily sustain life. The soil in and along the edges of the narrow trenches and ditches could produce enough food to supply a small community, if it was handled right. It was then that I began to realize that this place could have been doing just that for some of the ancient Indians who lived around here centuries ago.

"Do you know what this place is?" Monica said as she stood looking out over the plateau.

I looked at her. There was a glow on her face and her eyes were filled with excitement. She didn't wait for me to answer.

"This is the field of an ancient tribe of Indians who probably lived here over six hundred years ago."

"What makes you think so?" I asked as much to confirm what I believed as to understand what she was telling me.

"Look. What looks like trenches and ditches to us, were probably shallow irrigation cannels providing water to the ground on either side. The channels seem to run fairly straight. They run from over near that cliff, outward in all directions."

"That would mean that the source of the water is over there by the cliff," I said as I pointed toward the gray stone cliff.

"Yes. Remember that piece of jewelry that was found in Sam's pocket?" Monica asked.

"Sure. What about it?"

"My best guess is that it came from around here."

"What makes you think so?"

"The ancient people who lived here would have worshiped the sun and water. The design of that piece of jewelry is typical of the kind of jewelry that those people would have made. I think it is a replica of one of their larger symbols of worship, probably the sun."

I found what she was saying as very interesting. I also noticed that the sun was beginning to set. We would have to set up camp very soon, or we would be setting up camp in the dark.

"Let's get organized for the night. We can check this all out in the morning," I suggested.

"Okay. How about setting up camp over there," she said as she pointed to a place that looked very inviting to my weary bones.

We led the horses to a grassy area that had a small water hole. After hobbling them so they would not wonder off too far, we built a small fire. Monica prepared dinner while I stowed away our supplies and laid out our sleeping bags.

After a good meal, we relaxed on the sleeping bags. It had already turned dark. I looked up at the stars. The sky was full of them. It was hard to believe that there were so many. It was quiet and peaceful. The night air was cool. It was easy to see why the ancient people would want to live here.

It had been a long hard day. Monica curled up beside me and instantly fell asleep. I thought about standing watch for a while, but didn't think it was necessary. After all, we had a hard time finding this place. No one would be able to find it at night. It wasn't long before I drifted off into a deep restful sleep.

# CHAPTER FOURTEEN

It was still dark when I woke. The sky off to the east was beginning to show a little light, but off to the west it was still pretty dark. I'm not sure what it was that woke me, but I had a strange feeling that we were not alone. Something, or someone, was on the plateau with us. I was sure of it.

I sat up and looked at Monica. She had her back to me and she was still sound asleep. I slowly looked around. It was light enough that I could make out the silhouettes of the horses against the eastern skyline, but that was about it. They seemed to be undisturbed. If anyone was around, they would not be standing so quietly.

I laid back down, but found it difficult to go back to sleep. I had always trusted my senses, and they were telling me that something was out there. It was no time for me to ignore them. They had never let me down before.

I slid my hand under my bedroll and wrapped my fingers around the pistol I had hidden there. I sat up again, only this time with the gun in my hand. Once again I scanned the area.

When I looked toward the horses, I noticed that two of them had their heads up and their ears pointed toward the face of the cliff. The other two showed no sign of anything that should alert them to any kind of danger.

I looked toward the face of the cliff, but it was too dark to see anything. Whatever it was that had caught the interest of the horses, I could not see or hear.

Suddenly, the other two horses raised their heads and looked in the same direction. I knew something was over there, but what it was I couldn't say.

I reached out and lightly touched Monica on the shoulder. She raised her head and turned to look over her shoulder at me. Before she had a chance to say anything, I put my finger over my mouth so she would know to be quiet.

"We have company," I whispered softly as I pointed toward the cliff.

She turned and looked in the direction I had pointed. She was looking hard in an effort to see what was out there. Monica looked back at me and shook her head to indicate that she could not see anything.

"Something's over there.  Look at the horses," I whispered.

She looked at the horses, then looked in the direction they were looking. She turned to look at me.

"I don't see anything," she whispered.

"Here, take this," I whispered as I handed her the pistol.

"Where are you going?"

"I'm going to find out what's over there."

I rolled back over and picked up the rifle that I had laid next to my sleeping bag. Crouching down, I quickly moved into one of the shallow ditches. Keeping as low as possible, I moved quickly and quietly toward the cliff.

As I moved closer, I thought I saw something move, but I couldn't be sure. I readied myself for whatever might be there, but before I could make out what it was, it was gone. It had no shape, no form. It was just a movement in the darkness.

Suddenly, I heard what sounded like something splashing through water. I looked in the direction that the sound had come from, but could see nothing. The more I thought about what I had heard, the more I was convinced that it sounded more like someone, or something, running through a puddle.

I squatted down while I continued to scan the area for anything that moved. As I looked back toward the horses, I noticed that they had their heads down again. I was sure that whatever had disturbed them was now gone. At least, it had moved far enough away that the horses were no longer concerned about it.

As I returned to our camp, the sun was beginning to light up the area. It would not be long and I would be able to see anything that moved.

When I arrived back at our camp, Monica was kneeling on her sleeping bag, the gun still in her hands. She lowered the gun as soon as she was sure it was me. I could tell from the look on her face that she had been scared.

"It's all right," I said with a smile in the hope of easing her fears.

"What was it? Did you see anything?"

"No. All I saw was a shadow. I couldn't tell what it was. It could have been a coyote, a big jackrabbit, almost anything. I'll go see if I can find any tracks after breakfast."

"I'm not sure I like it here," she said as she looked up at me.

I had no difficulty understanding how she felt. I wasn't all that sure I liked it here, either.

"I think we need to stay here long enough to check out the plateau. If we don't find anything, we'll move on. Okay?"

"Okay," she replied reluctantly.

"I'm sorry. I'm acting like a scared child. I should know better. There's always a logical explanation for everything. It's just that it's not always easy to find or figure out. We'll stay here as long as we need to," she said looking up at me.

"Hey, this place makes me a little nervous, too. I'm not used to this. I'm a city boy, remember."

Monica smiled at me. I could see my effort to make light of our situation made her feel at least a little more comfortable. I wasn't sure if it helped me or not.

Monica put the gun down and stood up. She stepped up in front of me and put her hands on my shoulders. Holding the rifle in one hand, I reached around behind her with my other hand and pulled her up against me.

"I know you will protect me," she whispered as she looked up at me.

I smiled down at her. I sure hoped she was right.

"I'll sure try," I whispered as she drew my face closer to hers.

Our lips met in a long, passionate kiss. Her lips were warm and her body felt nice pressed tightly against me. She was so passionate and sexy that she could almost make me forget where we were and why we were here.

After our kiss, she looked up at me and whispered, "I'll fix breakfast if you build a fire."

"You got a deal, lady," I whispered as I took my arm from around her narrow waist.

Monica let go of me and went over to our supplies to get something for breakfast while I built a fire. As the flames began to spread among the tinder of the fire, my thoughts turned to what Monica had said.

Even legends have some basis in fact. Everything had an explanation, no matter how bizarre it might seem. It was just that sometimes it was hard, if not impossible to find. What I had heard and what I had seen could have been almost anything. It could have been an animal or a person. The one thing that I needed to know was which one.

I had no experience tracking people, or animals, but I would certainly know the difference once I found the tracks. As soon as we were finished with breakfast, I would go looking for tracks. I had to know if there was someone else on the plateau. If there was, who was it?

As soon as breakfast was ready, we sat down to eat. The sun was up and it was looking like it was going to be a hot day, bright and sunny. As I ate, I tried to remember what I had learned as a Boy Scout about tracks and tracking. I could remember a few things, but I was sure that I had forgotten more than I could remember.

"What are you thinking about? You look so serious," Monica asked.

I looked up at her. I could see the concerned look in her beautiful cobalt blue eyes. They were not only beautiful, they often told me what was on her mind.

"I was thinking about Sam."

"What about him?"

"He was a very smart man, and clever as well. He gave us a map of sorts that helped us find this place, which means he has been here before. He gave us a clue as to what he had found with the ancient piece of jewelry. And he warned us."

"What do you mean, "he warned us"?"

"What other possible reason would he have to give all these complicated clues if he wasn't worried about you? These clues were for you, and you alone."

"I don't understand."

"Think about it. You were the one person he felt he could trust. He also must have felt that he knew you as well, if not better, than anyone else. He must have felt that he knew how your mind works. Otherwise, he would not have left you the clues that he did, and in the way he did.

"He knew that if anything happened to him, you would be the most likely person to try to pick up where he left off and to find out what happened to him. He also knew that you would be in danger if anyone figured out that you might know something."

"I see what you mean," she said as she looked down at her food.

"Eat up. It's going to be a long day. The first order of business is to find some tracks from our early morning visitor," I said.

We finished our breakfast and cleaned up our campsite. The plateau was big, but the area where we had heard our visitor was not so big that we couldn't cover it on foot.

As soon as we were ready, I picked up the rifle and pointed in the general direction that I thought we should go.

We left the horses hobbled near the camp and set off toward the face of the cliff that overlooked the plateau. It was from that direction that I had heard the sounds of our visitor and had seen the shadows.

Monica took hold of my free hand and walked beside me. The feel of her soft warm hand in mine reminded me of how much she meant to me. It also reminded me that I had a responsibility to look out for her and protect her from harm.

I kept my eyes moving in an effort to take in anything that didn't seem normal. Around here there was very little that seemed normal to me. I was not used to being in a place like this, but I was adjusting to it.

My attention was suddenly drawn toward a long narrow opening in the face of the cliff. The sun had made it stand out. I was sure that if we had come by much later, the crack would look like a thin line in the rock wall. I was sure that it matched one of the photos we had copied.

"Nick?"

"Yeah?"

"Look at this."

Monica was looking down at the ground in front of her. I looked down, then knelt down to get a closer look. There on the ground in front of me, in the soft wet dirt, was a footprint. It was not just a footprint, but it was the footprint of a barefoot child, or small woman.

"This is a fairly fresh footprint," I said as I looked up at Monica.

"Do you suppose that someone lives up here?" she asked as she looked around.

"I haven't seen any kind of a house or shelter where they might live, but it would certainly be possible. After all, there is water and good grass up here. I would think it was possible that someone might even raise sheep or goats here."

"But how would they get them up here?"

"For one, they could always get up here the same way we got here. But I would be willing to bet that there's another way up here," I said as I looked around.

"What makes you think that?"

"We haven't seen any animals up here, yet they have been here. Look here," I said as I pointed to a print in the dirt.

"If I remember right, that looks like the hoof print of a goat or sheep."

"Mountain sheep?"

"Possibly, but I think some kind of domestic sheep. I think we should check out that narrow opening in the rocks. It looks like one of our photos."

I took Monica's hand and led her toward the narrow opening in the face of the cliff. Before we entered the opening, I took a moment to look around. I wanted to be sure that we were not being followed. I could see nothing but our horses enjoying the rich green grass.

Once inside, we found ourselves in what looked like a tunnel. We could not see very far back into the tunnel because it was dark. We had not expected to find the tunnel and didn't think to bring flashlights with us.

"I think we better check this out, but we need some light in here," I said.

"What do you want to do?"

"I think we should come back when we're prepared to go deep into the tunnel."

"I guess that sounds like a good idea," Monica agreed, but sounded unsure of herself.

We turned around and walked out of the tunnel. As soon as we were outside, I stopped and looked back at the entrance. It had all the earmarks of a natural cave. It could come out on the other side of the mountain, or dead end in just a few feet beyond the entrance. I wanted to know which.

I looked down at the ground. I couldn't say for sure, but it looked almost as if the ground had been brushed or racked over with a broom or some kind of brush, maybe with branches from a bush. If that was the case, then someone was trying to hide their tracks. The only tracks going into the cave that were clear, were the tracks Monica and I had just made. There was no doubt in my mind that this cave was a top priority for us. A complete investigation of this cave was in order.

As we began walking back toward our camp, I scanned the part of the plateau that I could see. At first I didn't notice anything different, but then I noticed that the horses were looking toward the west. Their ears were pointed and their heads were held high as if they were trying to figure out what was over there.

A quick look around revealed a shallow trench just off to our left. It ran from the face of the cliff out across the plateau in a straight line. I grabbed Monica by the arm and quickly led her to it.

I half expected her to resist me, but she came along without any hesitation. As soon as we were in the shallow trench, I dropped to my knees. Monica dropped down beside me.

"Nick?" she whispered.

"We've got company."

Monica didn't move. She just looked at me.

I slowly pulled the hammer of the rifle back, cocking the gun. I moved up to the rim of the trench and looked out toward the horses. They had not moved. They were still looking off toward the west.

"Do you see anything?" Monica asked in a whisper.

"Not yet, but there's something just to the west of our camp. The horses look a little nervous."

I continued to watch in the hope of seeing who or what was there. I could only think of two possibilities. One was that whoever had been here last night, or early this morning, was still here. That thought didn't seem to bother me that much. After all, we had found footprints in the mud of a small person. I doubted that the person who made the footprints was any real danger to us. After all, he had the chance to do us in last night while we were sleeping and didn't take it.

The second possibility gave me more to think about. If we were being followed, I was reasonably certain that we were in a lot of danger, especially if those following us had found the bodies of our guide and Morris.

My mind was going a hundred miles an hour in an effort to come up with an idea. Since I could not see anyone, I decided that we should go to our campsite as quickly as possible. We could take cover in one of the trenches or channels if we had to, otherwise, we should break camp and move closer to the cliff. From there we could hold off any attack against us.

"Come on", I said as I grabbed Monica by the hand.

She didn't hesitate. She was on her feet and running beside me toward our camp. When we got to the camp, I dropped down on my knees. Pressing the rifle against my shoulder, I again scanned the area over the top of my rifle. At first, I didn't see anything, then I saw something move in the thick grass about two hundred yards west of the camp.

I waited and held my breath. If we had been followed, we were out in the open. In order to avoid being seen, we would have to crawl along the trench to the face of cliff. That was a very long way to crawl.

Suddenly, I saw it. A large coyote bounded out of the trench and stopped. He was looking at the horses as if he was surprised to see them there. If the coyote spent a lot of time on the plateau, he would have good reason to be surprised to see the horses.

I lowered the rifle from my shoulder and sat back on my heels as I let out a sigh of relief. As I looked at Monica, I could see the strange look on her face. It was clear that she was wondering what was going on.

"It's a coyote," I said with a grin.

She looked at me in disbelief, then rose up to look out across the plateau. A smile came over her face as she realized that a coyote had frightened us. She turned around and sat down on the ground.

I turned around and sat down beside her. She reached over and put her hand on my leg. We smiled at each other as we caught our breath.

"I never realized that a coyote could frighten me so," Monica said.

"It wasn't the coyote that frightened you. It was not knowing what we were going to encounter that frightened you. But I wouldn't get too comfortable. It was a coyote this time, but we don't know what it will be next time," I reminded her.

She looked at me. I could tell from the look in her eyes that she understood. She knew as well as I that as long as we were here, as long as we were looking for the same thing that Sam had been looking for, our lives were in danger.

I leaned my rifle against one of the packs for our horses and built a small fire. A cup of coffee sounded very good about now. I always think better with a cup of coffee in my hand, and now was a good time to think.

It was also a time to plan. The more I thought about what we had come here to do, the more convinced I became that someone was going to try to stop us.

As I poured us each a cup of coffee, I began to review everything that had happened to us. I also spent a little time going over in my mind everyone that seemed to have anything to do with Sam's trips to the Superstition Mountains.

My first thoughts were of Russell Martin. He was convinced that his brother had been murdered. Based on his brother's education and ability, and the manner in which he died, he had every right to think that. And I had no reason to doubt his motives for wanting to find out what actually happened at the cave.

My thoughts turned to Professor William Campbell. From what I knew about him, he was ambitious, cold and calculating. He struck me as the type who would do anything to increase his prestige in the academic community, and I mean anything. I had no idea what his background was other than his education as an anthropologist. However, it was clear that he liked the things money could buy, the fancy cars and expensive clothes, for example.

Campbell seemed like the most likely suspect. Although I didn't like him, he seemed to have the drive and the desire to get what he was after. I also got the feeling that he didn't care whose toes he stepped on in the process. I wasn't so sure if he would kill to get what he wanted, but then murder had been committed for very little.

As I thought of those who had been on the first expedition, I remembered Professor Paul Garvey. For some reason, I had put him in the back of my mind. Yet, he had as much to gain as any of the others in the success of that expedition. He also had as much to lose.

It was then that I realized that I knew very little about him. Monica had not mentioned him, other than to say that he had been on the first expedition. But I recalled Russell Martin telling me that he had an argument with Sam just before they were to go into the mountains. The next thing that happened was Professor Martin was killed in the cave, and the trip was ended.

"What are you thinking about?" Monica said, interrupting my thoughts.

"I was just thinking about Professor Garvey."

"What about him?"

"I've never met him, have I?" I asked as I poured a little more coffee in my cup.

"No. I don't think so."

"What can you tell me about him?"

"No much, really " Monica answered. "I guess no one knows much about him."

"Why's that?"

"I don't know. I guess it's because he sort of keeps to himself. He never attends any kind of dinners or banquets held at the university. He attends lectures by some of the other professors occasionally, especially lectures that were given by Sam. He never seems to do anything to make waves."

"What do you mean by that?"

"At staff meetings, for example, he never says much of anything. You know, when I think about it, I think Sam was his only friend."

"How did he get along with the rest of the staff?"

"Okay, I guess."

"Did you ever see him argue a point, or get upset with anyone over something he was working on?"

"No. I remember one time when there was some discussion on cuts in the budget for the history department, his face got red. I think it was the first time I ever saw him get mad, but he didn't say anything. It's funny, but he's like the mouse in the corner. You never really notice him. It's as if he is never there," she said as she looked at me.

I thought about her description of Professor Garvey. He never argued about cuts in the budget, something that would certainly have affected him directly. Yet, he got into an argument with his best, and possibly his only friend, over where to start their expedition. Somehow that didn't make sense to me.

"Do you want any more coffee?"

Monica's question disturbed my thoughts again. I looked over at her and saw that she was looking at me. The expression on her face indicated to me that she was wondering what was going on in my mind.

"What?"

"I asked if you want any more coffee?"

"No. I think we should move our camp to a safer place. We are sitting out here in the open," I said as I poured the remaining liquid from my cup on the fire.

"That's a good idea. Where do you want to move it?"

"Over near the face of the cliff, near the cave. If we run into trouble, the cave could provide us with good cover."

"Sounds good to me," she replied, then drank down the rest of her coffee.

We worked together to gather up the horses and our supplies. Once we were ready, we moved closer to the cave. From there we would be able see most of the plateau, and would be able to see anyone who might approach.

# CHAPTER FIFTEEN

We set up our new camp only some twenty to twenty-five yards from the entrance to the cave. We found a place that was slightly higher than the general level of the surrounding ground giving us a good view of almost the entire plateau.

The area we had selected for our campsite was shaped like a half circle with the straight side against the face of the cliff. The front side, or curved side, had what could only be described as a low wall around it with an opening near the face of the cliff only a short distance from the cave entrance.

I quickly determined that this place would be fairly easy to defend, if it should become necessary. There was even enough room that we could keep the horses inside the walled area, at least for a short time. I had hobbled them outside in an area that was rich with grass and fresh water in order to conserve the water and grass inside the walled area in case we needed to keep them in close.

The more I looked at our new campsite and the surrounding area, the more I realized it may very well have been used as a place for ancient Indians to guard the entrance to the cave. It would allow anyone standing guard to see who was coming from some distance. From here, I could see almost the entire plateau. It would also provide protection for the defending force to hold off their enemy if they should come under attack by any of their enemies.

"Monica, this looks like it might have been a guard post a hundred of years ago," I said as I stood on the low wall and looked out over the plateau.

"It could have been, but a lot longer ago than a hundred years. The ancient Indians who lived in this part of the world built some pretty elaborate fortification to protect them from their enemies. They often built earthworks around their villages. This could very well have been one, only I'm sure that the wall was much higher then."

I continued to think about the place as I helped Monica prepare our campsite. I spent a good deal of the time gathering firewood while she stacked and stored supplies.

Once we were settled in at our new campsite, we prepared ourselves for the trip into the cave. We put a few things to snack on in haversacks and checked our flashlights.

"You ready?"

"Yes. Nick?"

"Yes?"

"Do you think we will find what Sam was looking for in there?"

"I don't know, honey. But I do know that we have to try to find it."

Monica nodded her head in agreement and forced a smile. I reached out and took hold of her hand. As we started toward the entrance of the cave, I squeezed her hand gently to let her know that I understood how she was feeling.

We stopped for a second or two at the entrance of the cave to look it over. It also gave us a chance to take a deep breath. I could tell by the way she held my hand that she was as nervous as I was about going into the cave. I couldn't blame her for that after what had happened at the last cave we were in.

I looked over at Monica and found her looking at me. I smiled, then turned on my flashlight. She turned hers on.

"Ready?"

"Yes," she replied nervously.

I winked and stepped forward into the cave. Monica held onto my hand as we slowly started into the cave.

As we moved deeper into the cave, we carefully scanned the walls, the floor and the ceiling of the cave with our lights. I couldn't help but remember the fine wire that we found in the other cave, and the dynamite attached to the end of it. I had no reason to believe that this cave was booby-trapped, but it certainly wouldn't hurt to be cautious.

There seemed to be one major difference in this cave over the last one we were in. Other than the fact that it was much bigger, the walls and ceilings of this cave were relatively smooth. There were no large cracks and crevasses in the walls or ceilings.

I hadn't realized it until I turned around to look back, but the cave had a slight curve to it. When I looked back I could no longer see the entrance. Also, the deeper we went into the cave, the more I was beginning to think of it more like a tunnel than a cave.

"Nick, look at this," Monica said, her voice showing a hint of excitement.

I looked at the spot on the wall where Monica was shinning her flashlight. I moved closer and shined my flashlight on the same spot in order to get a better look.

There on the wall, scratched in the rock, was what appeared to be hieroglyphics. It looked like a drawing of a stick man and some animals that looked like they might be sheep or goats.

"What do you make of it?" I asked.

"There is no telling how old this is, but it looks like a sheepherder was here. There are some other symbols here, but I can't make them out. My best guess would be that a sheepherder might have taken shelter in this cave at one time, possibly hundreds of years ago. While he was here, he scratched these in the wall to tell what happened here."

"Shelter from what?"

"I'm not sure. I can't make out enough to know why he was here. It could have been that he came in here to protect himself and his flock from the weather or from some enemy. There's no way of knowing without being able to make out more of what is here," she said as she continued to study the hieroglyphics.

"Let's move on. We can take another look at it later," I suggested.

Once again we began moving deeper into the cave. I continued to watch for any danger, but I also watched for more hieroglyphics. I knew it was a long shot, but they could give us some clue to what we might find further in.

I stopped and took a minute to study the floor of the cave for tracks. Monica shined her light down to give me more light.

"Anything?"

"No. There are tracks in here, but I can't make them out. The rock floor is just too hard for anything to leave a clear track."

I stood up and we pressed on. We could have made better time if we were not being so careful. I would rather live than find some lost civilization that had died off hundreds of years ago just in time to join them. I didn't like the idea of joining them in the happy hunting grounds. I preferred alive to dead any day.

I don't know how far we had gone into the cave, but we had gone some distance when the cave suddenly opened up into a large room like area. It was unbelievably large. The ceiling must have been close to forty feet high at the highest point. It was shaped like the inside of a dome. The room looked to be at least eighty feet in diameter. I was unable to tell just how big it was, but it was big.

"What do you make of this?" I asked Monica.

"I don't know," she replied as she looked around.

"Do you think that this was carved in the rock by the ancient Indians?" I asked as I looked around.

"I suppose it's possible, but it would have taken them ages to do it."

"What do we do now?" I asked knowing full well that she was the expert here.

"I think we should stay together and look for passages, or tunnels or hieroglyphics that might tell us more about who had been here before us," she replied.

"Which way?"

"Let's go around to the left and see where it takes us," she suggested.

"Any particular reason for going left?"

"No."

"Could it be because most right-handed people would go to the left?"

"Is that true?" she asked.

"I don't know. It's just that I would have picked going left, too," I replied with a grin.

"I guess that's as good a reason as any," she said with a slight laugh in her voice.

Monica led off, moving along the wall to the left with me at her side. We had gone maybe twenty feet, maybe less when we noticed what looked like the entrance to another tunnel. We stopped and shined our flashlights into the tunnel. We could not see very far down it, but it looked like it might go back in quite a ways.

"Well, what do you think?" I asked Monica.

She shined her flashlight on the wall around the entrance. I was sure she was looking for something, but I wasn't sure what.

"Here," she said as she stepped closer to the wall where she was pointing her flashlight.

Painted on the wall were several figures in a circle. In the center of the circle was what looked like it could have been a painting of a fire. Several of the figures had what appeared to be headdresses. It was hard to tell, as the painting was old and faded. One thing that did strike me as interesting was that the figures in the circle were not stick figures like the ones we had seen in the tunnel when we first entered.

"This looks like a council meeting. I can't say for sure, but the tunnel could very well led back to another room, possibly a council room of some kind," she explained.

"What do you make of the fact that the figures are different from the ones near the entrance?"

"I think this painting is actually older."

"You want to go check out this tunnel?"

"I don't know, do you?"

"I think we should finish checking out this room first," I suggested.

"Okay."

Without further comment, we continued along the wall of the large room. We hadn't gone very far when we came to some more hieroglyphics. It was a rather large drawing this time, but it was much different from the others. Even I could understand it.

The drawings showed a large number of figures. Some wore headdresses, while others wore helmets much like the Spanish soldiers wore in the fifteen hundreds. Many of the figures were lying down indicating to me that they were dead. There were horses both standing and lying down as well.

From the size of the drawing, it was clear to me that a great battle had taken place. It apparently had been between the ancient Indians who lived here and the Spaniards who had come here to conquer the land. On closer examination, most of the figures that were lying down had Spanish helmets, indicating to me that the Indians had defeated the Spaniards but at great cost. The only thing that I didn't get from the picture was where this great battle had taken place.

"I'm not the expert, but from the looks of the drawing, it seems clear to me that there was one hell of battle somewhere near here," I said to Monica as I continued to look at the painting.

"I think you're right. It was between the Spaniards and the Indians."

"I noticed that there were several designs above the drawing that looked like suns. There was at least four that I could make out. What do you make of them? I would call them suns." I asked Monica.

"I'm not a hundred percent sure, but it would tend to indicate that the battle lasted several days."

"Any idea who won? My guess would be the Indians."

"I would say that the Indians probably won," she agreed.

"Any ideas as to what the fight was about?"

"No," she said as she turned and looked around the room. "I get the feeling that this is The Great Room."

"Yeah, it is a pretty good size place," I agreed.

"No, silly. I mean 'The Great Room'. The Great Room was supposed to be a place where all the members of the tribe would gather to tell stories, make decisions that affected the entire tribe, and to hold special celebrations and meetings. Sort of a gathering place to talk and share information, as well as celebrate important dates or events."

"Oh," I replied feeling rather stupid at the moment.

"There are probably a number of rooms off this room where supplies were stored, treasures were stored, where smaller ceremonies were held, and where the chiefs met to discuss problems and make decisions, even hold trials," she explained.

"You may have hit the nail on the head," I commented.

"What?" she asked, a little confused by my remark.

"You said, "Where treasures were stored"."

"But where?"

"That I don't know, but with some time and effort, I think we just might be able to figure it out."

"What do we do now?"

"We continue to check out The Great Room. When we're done with that, we'll go back to camp. Then starting again tomorrow, we'll start checking out each room we find, one at a time."

During the next few hours, we found what appeared to be five tunnels to five rooms. Each one of them had a hieroglyph near the entrance. As best we could figure it, the hieroglyphics gave us some indication as to what the room was used for.

We also found several large drawings around the room, six in all, plus one additional small one that was not located near a tunnel. The large ones seemed to depict important events in the lives of the people who had lived there. Everything seemed to be in balance.

When we finished going around the outside edge of the room, we walked toward the center. When we got to the center of the room, we found what appeared to have been a large fire pit. We soon discovered that it was of an unusual shape. It was round in the center, but it had several points like those on a compass that pointed out away from the circle.

"I wonder how they kept from suffocating when they built a fire in here," I said as I looked down at the fire pit.

"I don't know." Monica replied.

I got to thinking that it was a long ways from the entrance of the cave to the center of this room. To build a fire anywhere near the size of the fire pit would make it almost impossible for any human being to breath in here.

As I walked around the fire pit, I thought I felt a slight draft. There was air flowing through here, but I couldn't be sure which way it was flowing. I needed a match or a torch to find out.

If the airflow was up, that would mean that there was enough of a crack in the rock above The Great Room that the smoke would work its way out of the cave. If it was coming from someplace else, that could mean that there was at least one of the tunnels that had access to the outside, other than the one that we had used to come in.

"Can you feel it?" I asked as I tried to figure out which way the draft was moving.

"Feel what?" Monica replied.

"Wet your finger and hold it up?"

Monica looked at me as if I was a little strange, but did as I told her. In the dim light of our flashlights, I could see the surprised look on her face.

"There's a draft through here," she said as she looked at me and smiled.

"Yeah, but from where to where. This cave has more than one entrance, or at least it has a way for the air to pass through."

"Do you suppose that one of those five tunnels goes outside?" she asked.

"It's certainly possible. It might be how the person that visited us last night got here. It may be how they get their sheep or goats up here, too."

"That might explain why we never saw any tracks in the canyon we took to get up here.

"It might," I agreed. "We can check that out tomorrow when we start checking out each of the tunnels," I suggested.

"Nick, have you taken a real good look at this fire pit?" Monica asked as she looked at the pit.

"Yeah, I guess. It's a fire pit. What about it?"

"It has six points coming out from the center."

I took another look at it. She was right. It had six points coming out from the center.

"I see. Do you have any idea what it means?"

"No, but I'm sure it has some significance," Monica replied.

"Well, I think we should return to camp. It's probably getting close to sunset. We've been in here a long time."

I took Monica by the hand. I had a pretty good idea where the tunnel was that would lead to the outside, but it was hard to see from the center of the Great Room using just a couple of flashlights. I shined my flashlight in the direction I thought would be toward the tunnel. My hesitation must have told Monica that I wasn't sure of myself. She squeezed my hand.

"Are we lost in here?" she asked in a whisper.

"No. I just need to get my bearings."

As soon as I was sure of which tunnel we needed to use, I started toward it. We soon found ourselves in the long tunnel that had brought us into the Great Room. We moved along much faster than when we came in.

I don't know what Monica was thinking about as we walked through the tunnel, but I was thinking about what we had seen. There was something that kept nagging at my mind. Something that just didn't seem right, but I couldn't put my finger on it. Right up until we stepped out into the evening light I continued to try to figure out what it was that was not as I thought it should be.

When we stepped out of the cave into the light, we shut off our flashlights. The sun was just beginning to set in the west. The sky was full of colors as the sun reflected off the high thin clouds.

Although I was seeing the beautiful sunset, my mind was cluttered with a dozen random thoughts. My thoughts seemed to be running into each other to the point that I was unable to sort them out and think of any one of them long enough to examine it.

My thoughts were suddenly disturbed by the howl of a lone coyote off in the distance. I listened briefly to see if I might hear the return call of its mate, but I heard nothing.

My mind began to absorb the peace and tranquility of my surroundings. It was easy to see why the ancient Indians had lived here. It was quiet and undisturbed by the usual daily routine that had become a part of my life. It was a beautiful place, but I doubted that the Indians who had lived here would have totally agreed with my assessment. In their time, I'm sure it was a daily struggle just to survive day to day. However, their counterparts that live on the desert floor would have had a much more difficult time surviving.

"I knew there was something about that fire pit that looked familiar," Monica said as she held out the fax of the ancient piece of jewelry that had been found on Sam's body. "It has the same general shape with the same number of points as this."

I looked at the fax, then at Monica. She was right, it was an important symbol, but what did it mean? What significance did it have? I even wondered if that was what I was having difficulty understanding. Somehow it didn't seem to be.

There was something else that was bothering me. Something else that just didn't seem to fit in the total picture. It was as if something was missing that should be there, but I couldn't figure out what it was.

"Nick, are you all right?"

"Oh. Yeah, I'm fine. I'm having trouble putting this all together. I keep thinking that something is missing."

"I know what you mean, but to me it's more like there's something there that doesn't belong. Maybe if we have something to eat and get a good night's rest, we'll be able to figure it out," she suggested.

"Good idea. I'll get a fire going."

I built a small fire pit in the center of our camp, then built a fire. As soon as I had it going good, Monica brought over a pan and began fixing dinner. I moved aside and sat down on the wall that surrounded the front half of our campsite.

As the light grew dim, I watched the horses eat the rich grass. They seemed undisturbed by their strange surroundings. They were content to enjoy the fresh spring water and grass.

As I looked out over the plateau, I remembered the visitor that had been close to our camp last night. It reminded me that we were not alone up here, high above the desert floor. Although we had not been attacked, and no attempt had been made to harm us or to contact us, I felt it would be a good idea if we brought the horses in closer. If we had company tonight, we would stand a better chance of knowing someone or something was close with the horses inside the half circle of our campsite.

"Dinner's ready," Monica called out.

I took one last look around before I walked back to the fire. While we ate our dinner, I told her about my plan to bring the horses inside the circle of our campsite. She seemed to think that it was a good idea.

After dinner, I rounded up the horses and tied them to a picket line inside the half circle. When everything was done that needed to be done, I returned to the wall.

"What are you doing," Monica asked as she sat down beside me.

"Just looking out at the night."

Monica leaned back against me. I wrapped my arms around her and held her as we sat quietly looking out over the plateau and listening to the sounds of the night. It was interesting the different sounds you can hear in a place like this. We could hear the horses as they chomped on the grass; the sound of a distant jet as it sped across the sky to some unknown destination, and the call of a lone coyote.

"It's so peaceful up here," Monica sighed.

I didn't respond to her comment. It was peaceful now, but just the other day someone had tried to kill us. The tranquility of this place could lull a person into a false sense of security.

Even though I was enjoying the moment, I had no doubt that it would not be long before it would be discovered that Morris had failed to kill us and prevent us from continuing our search for the killer of Sam Kishler. I was sure that whoever had killed Sam, would try to do the same thing to us.

Monica yawned. I knew that it had been a long day for her. We needed to get our rest as tomorrow promised to be another long day.

"Come on. We better get some rest," I suggested.

We stood up and walked back to our sleeping bags. We laid down and she curled up against me. It was only a matter of minutes before she was asleep.

I laid looking up at the stars. I reached down alongside my bedroll to make sure that my rifle was where I could put my hands on it if I needed it in a hurry. My pistol was next to my head, under the saddle I was using for a pillow.

I took one last look at the horses to make sure they were calm. They seemed to be sleeping. I closed my eyes and drifted off into a restful sleep.

# CHAPTER SIXTEEN

I woke when there was just a hint of light in the eastern sky. It looked like it was going to be a beautiful day, and no one would want to miss this sunrise. The sky was clear and the morning star was still bright.

I heard a horse move and looked toward them. Two of the horses seemed a little nervous as if they had heard something, or smelled something that was unfamiliar to them. The other two appeared to be sleeping.

I glanced over at Monica and found her sound asleep on her side, her back to me. I slowly rolled away from her in the hope of not disturbing her rest. I picked up my rifle, stood up and moved over to the wall.

Keeping down behind the wall, I looked out into the darkness. It was still too dark to see anything clearly, so I strained to listen in the hope of hearing whatever it was that had made the two horses nervous. I heard nothing.

After several minutes of looking and listening, I felt it was safe to relax. I moved up on top of the wall and sat down. Over the years I had often sat in the pre-dawn hours in my bedroom window and watched the sun come up. It was a time to let my mind wander over the events of a case I was working on. It had proven to be very helpful on a number of occasions. The quiet of this beautiful, peaceful morning might be just the thing I needed to get some answers, and clear my mind. Laying the rifle across my lap, I let my mind wander over the events of the past few days.

My thoughts quickly passed through all the events that had led up to yesterday, and what we had seen in "The Great Room", as Monica had called it. I remembered the six large drawings that appeared to be almost equally spaced around

The Great Room. There were the six points that appeared to be equally spaced around the fire pit and for the most part pointed at different tunnels. And there was the ancient jewelry with its six arrows that pointed out from the center and looked very much like the fire pit. Then there were the six smaller hieroglyphics. There was one placed next to each of the five tunnels that spread out from The Great Room, and the one placed almost perfectly between two of the tunnels.

"Wait a minute," I said out loud to myself.

I knew something was wrong. There was six of everything except for the tunnels. There were only five tunnels. Now I was confused.

I racked my brain to remember what it was that I really saw in The Great Room. There were six large drawings on the walls. They were equally spaced around the room. That seemed normal enough, so I felt I could dismiss those from my mind for the time being.

Secondly, there were five tunnels, plus the one we used to get into The Great Room. That made six, and six seemed to be the common number. Everything seemed to be in sync if there were six.

Then there were six small drawings, each one located just to the right of a tunnel, except for one. Each small drawing appeared to be there to describe what the tunnel led to, for example, the council room, the storage rooms, and so on. A couple of the drawings were hard to figure out what they meant. Again, there were six drawings. Everything seemed to be in order except for the one small drawing that seemed to be out of place. It was not next to a tunnel, and there were no drawings next to the main tunnel.

I tried to concentrate on that one drawing. It was then that I vaguely remembered that it was on the wall almost directly across from the tunnel that led us into The Great Room. I thought that was a little strange since all the rest were next to a tunnel entrance, but who knows why people do what they do. There must have been a very logical reason for the position of the drawing, at least logical to those who drew it, but I could not figure out what it could be. There were still six of them, and that seemed to fit the pattern.

Something filed deep in the recesses of my mind silently told me that although everything seemed to be in order, it was not. There was still something that was not right. The picture was not complete, something was still missing.

I don't know how long I thought about it, but the whinny of one of the horses suddenly caused me to look up. I noticed that all of the horses were looking out toward the plateau. The sky was getting light and I could see for some distance now, but could not see anything that would disturb the horses as I scanned the plateau.

Then I saw it. The lone coyote that we had seen before came bounding out of one of the trenches and crossed over into another. I watched him as he leisurely trotted across the plateau from one shallow trench to the next. He didn't seem to be in any hurry, but he did seem to have a destination in mind. He seemed pretty relaxed as his ears flopped and his tail bobbed as he casually trotted through the thick grass.

Suddenly, he stopped and looked off toward the west. His head and ears came up, and he tucked his tail down between his legs. Something had caught his attention, something that caused him to take notice.

I looked in the direction that the coyote was looking, but I couldn't see anything. As I looked back at the coyote, he broke into a run. He headed east and seemed to be going as fast as he could. I watched him until he ran behind a slight ridge and disappeared from sight.

I slid down behind the wall and drew my rifle up to my shoulder. Looking out over the top of my rifle, I slowly scanned the plateau trying to see what it was that had made the coyote run, but I still saw nothing. I continued to wait and watch. That coyote had run off for a reason. There was something out there that had frightened him, but what?

I heard Monica behind me as she got up and moved over to the wall next to me. As I glanced back over my shoulder toward her, I noticed that she was keeping down. She crawled the last few feet up beside me and looked out over the wall.

"What's going on?" she whispered.

"Nothing, so far. I saw our lone coyote out there this morning. Something startled him. He ran off that way," I said as I pointed in the direction the coyote had gone.

"What frightened him?"

"Don't know. Haven't seen a thing, so far."

Monica looked out over the plateau for several minutes. We didn't talk, just looked and listened. I was glad to have a second pair of eyes. I couldn't see that anything had changed.

"I don't see anything, either," she said as she looked over at me.

If anything had been out there, I was sure that we would have seen it. A quick glance at the horses gave me reason to relax a little. They no longer had their heads and ears up. They were either eating, or they had gone back to sleep.

"I don't know what was out there, but I think it's gone. It looks like it's going to be a beautiful day," I said as I looked up at the clear blue sky.

Monica smiled, then rolled over on her back and looked up. I immediately found myself staring at her. She was as beautiful a woman as they come. Even in jeans and a denim shirt, she looked sexy.

"I was thinking," she said interrupting my thoughts of her. "You haven't kissed me this morning."

"You're right. I'll have to do something about that."

I laid the rifle down and rolled over to her. As I leaned down over her, she reached out and wrapped her arms around my neck, pulling me down over her as our lips met. Our kiss was a long, passionate kiss, meant to show how much we loved each other.

She moaned softly as I rose up and looked down at her. We were both breathing heavily.

"Now that's what I call a good morning kiss," she sighed.

"Well, I thought you could have put a little more into it," I said smiling down at her.

"You did?"

"Yes. I did."

"Maybe you should try this one on and see if this is more to your liking," she said as she squeezed me around the neck and rolled me over on my back.

She rolled up over me and stretched out on top of me as she pressed her lips hard against mine. I wrapped my arms around her and held her to me. The feel of her firm body stretched out over me raised my desire for her rapidly. I instantly found myself sliding my hand over her back and over the snug jeans that covered her shapely bottom. She moaned softly as I lightly squeezed her butt through her jeans.

After a long hard kiss, she rose up and looked down at me. I smiled up and took a deep breath.

"Now that's what I call a good morning kiss," I said breathlessly.

"I could tell you liked it."

"And just how could you tell?"

"By the way you touch me," she whispered as she leaned back down for another kiss.

After another long hard kiss, she rose up again and rolled off me. She laid on her back and looked over at me. I smiled as I watched her breasts rise and fall with each breath she took, then I looked up at her face.

"I wish we were back at the place with the pool. I would like to have a bath," she whispered.

"Me, too."

"I suppose we better get a move on. What is it the cowboys say, 'We're burnin' daylight'?"

"Something like that," I said with a grin. "I'll get a fire started and make some coffee."

"I'm going to wash up," Monica said as she sat up.

I watched her as she stood up and walked over to the spring. After she left, I went to the fire pit we had built and rekindled the fire. I started the coffee, then went to the spring to wash up while Monica prepared breakfast.

The spring was about sixty feet from the fire pit. I knelt down at the small bucket size pool where the water bubbled up out of the ground. I scooped up some of the cool water and splashed it on my face. The water felt good. I repeatedly splashed water on my face until I felt refreshed and clean, then ran my wet hands through my hair.

I sat back on my heels and looked out over the plateau. I wasn't looking for anything special, just enjoying the view. The sun was full up in the sky, and the green grass looked rich and thick. It looked so peaceful and quiet.

I stood up and stretched as I turned around and looked back toward our fire. I expected to see Monica kneeling down by the fire cooking breakfast, but she was not there.

At first, I just looked around as if I was looking for nothing special, but it soon began to register in my mind that Monica was gone, she had disappeared. I could feel the panic start to build up in my chest. My heart began to pound so hard that I could feel it.

"Monica!" I yelled, but there was no answer.

Where was she? What had happened to her? My mind was going a mile a minute as I tried to understand what was happening.

I ran back to the fire pit. The eggs were burning in the pan, and the coffee was slowly boiling away. I kicked the pan off the fire and dumped over the coffeepot. She couldn't just vanish. She had to be close, but where?

I stopped and took in a deep breath. I had to get control of myself. I had to think if I was going to find her.

As I began to filter out the panic and began to think more clearly, I realized that she had to have been abducted. She would not just leave without saying something. Someone had to have taken her while I had my back turned, but who?

I had two thoughts come to mind. The first was that she had been abducted by whoever it was who was living up here on the plateau. We had seen the footprints of a child or small woman. Where there were children, there was bound to be adults, both males and females.

The second thought was that whoever had tried to stop us from coming here in the first place, had found Morris's body and was now here to finish the job. I had no basis for it, but my second choice seemed the most likely one.

A quick glance at my sleeping bag revealed that my rifle was gone. I also could see scrapes in the dirt. They had to be from Monica's boot as she was dragged off. The long gouges made by her boots lead right toward the entrance to the cave.

I knelt down on our sleeping bags and quickly looked for our handguns. I found Monica's first, then mine. I stuffed her smaller gun in my boot, then picked up a flashlight. With my gun in one hand, and my flashlight in the other, I started for the cave.

As I approached the entrance to the cave, I leaned up against the face of the cliff just to the side of the entrance. I listened in the hope of hearing something, anything that would tell me that she was still okay. I heard nothing.

I took a deep breath as I prepared to go into the cave to hunt for her. As I did, I wondered how anyone had been able to sneak up on us. Our campsite set higher than the surrounding area. I looked around for some clue as to how anyone could have gotten so close to us without being seen.

It was then that I noticed a narrow ditch that ran along the face of the cliff just on the other side of the entrance. I couldn't believe that I hadn't noticed it before. It would not be hard for someone to work their way right up to the entrance of the cave without being seen, especially at night. If they were quiet, even the horses would not know they were there.

I cursed myself for not having seen it before. Because I had not seen the ditch, I had left us vulnerable. I had put Monica in danger. Now I had to find her and get her back.

I looked down at the ground as I took a deep breath. There in the ground were the tracks from Monica's boots where she had been dragged into the cave.

After tucking my flashlight up under my arm, I checked to see that my gun was fully loaded. I also check Monica's gun and slipped it back into my boot. Holding my gun firmly in my hand, I quickly stepped inside the cave and pressed up against the wall. I looked into the darkness of the cave as I waited for my eyes to adjust to the darkness. The light from the outside would allow me to move deeper into the cave without the use of the flashlight. I knew that using the flashlight would give away my position, but I would eventually have to use it or stumble around without being able to see.

I began slowly moving deeper into the cave listening for any kind of sound, anything that would give me a hint as to where Monica might be found. It crossed my mind that she had been abducted so that I would come after her. I knew that this whole thing could be a trap, but what choice did I have. I had to find her, even if it was a trap.

I couldn't think about that now. I had to think of Monica, and how to get to her.

When I could no longer see the entrance of the cave, the cave had become so dark that I had to use my flashlight in order to see. I put my fingers over the lens to reduce the brightness of the light making it more difficult for anyone else to see. I spread my fingers just enough to give me enough light to see my way.

As I moved deeper into the tunnel, I began to notice a dim glow of light coming from in front of me. There was too much light for it to be coming from a flashlight, it had to be coming from something much brighter.

I worked my way closer to the light, until I no longer needed the flashlight. I shut it off and bent down to lay it on the floor at the base of the wall where I could find it if I should need it again.

I moved slowly along the wall. As I inched my way along the wall, The Great Room began to come into view. I was surprised to see the room cast in a glow of light.

I was still twenty or thirty feet from The Great Room as I worked my way around the bend in the tunnel. As the room came into view, I could see why the room was lighted. Setting around the edge of the large fire pit, were three large Coleman lanterns that filled the room with light.

But it was who was on the other side of the fire pit that concerned me. I could see Monica sitting on the edge of one of the star shaped points coming out from the fire pit. I could see that she was tied hand and foot, and that she had a gag over her mouth.

My first instinct was to run to her, to rip the gag off her mouth and untie her, but that would be not only foolish, it would be stupid. There was no doubt in my mind that this was a trap set up to get me, and she was the bait.

My mind filled with thoughts. Who had abducted her? If it was someone like Professor Campbell, he would have no need of me, but he might have need of Monica. If he didn't know where the treasure was, he might need her to help him find it. She was the expert on ancient Indians and their customs, but then he might be also. I didn't know where his field of expertise was.

It was time for me to do something. I had no plan in mind, but I knew that I had no choice but to show myself. To do anything else might cause Monica's abductors to kill her. My only hope was to get them to talk. If I could find out who was involved, I might be able to get us out of this alive.

"I'm coming out with my hands up," I called out to whoever might be listening.

I wasn't sure I was ready for this, but I couldn't think of any other way. As I stepped away from the wall, I noticed Monica was looking toward me. I wasn't sure if she could see me or not, but the look on her face told me that she was scared to death.

# CHAPTER SEVENTEEN

I raised my hands up above my head and started out of the tunnel into The Great Room. I had no idea what to expect, but I was hoping that whoever was there would not simply shoot me.

"I'll take that," I heard a voice from behind me say as I felt someone grab my gun and take it from my hand.

The voice of the person behind me was not familiar. I made no effort to turn around to see who was there. I stood still taking in what I could of the room without moving my head too much. I could see someone in the shadows of the tunnel off to my right, but I couldn't see who it was.

As I turned my head slightly to the left, I saw a short man with the features of an Indian standing in the entrance to one of the tunnels. He had a rifle in his hands and it was pointed at me. Based on what I had learned about the previous expeditions, I had the feeling that it was Juan Vasquez, the guide from the first trip Sam had made into these mountains.

"Well, if it isn't our illustrious Detective Nicholas McCord from Milwaukee."

I had no trouble recognizing that voice. I turned slowly to my right in time to see Professor Campbell step out of one of the tunnels and into the light. He was dressed much like I would have expected. He was in khaki pants and jacket like a great white hunter. He also had a self-satisfied grin on his face.

"I had a feeling you were in on this. I guess they don't pay you enough at the university," I said.

"I have pretty expensive tastes. This will allow me to indulge in those things I happen to appreciate," he said confidently.

"You may have expensive tastes and a good education, but you're just a common killer. You killed Sam for the oldest reason in the world, greed."

"I didn't actually do the killing," he commented as if not pulling the trigger somehow made him less of a murderer.

"Maybe not, but you hired the killer. That makes you as guilty as he is."

"It's too bad that no one will ever know, isn't it," he said as he stepped up in front of me. "Take him over there and tie him up," Campbell ordered Vasquez.

Vasquez walked over to me and poked me in the ribs with the end of his rifle barrel. I thought about swinging around and taking his rifle away from him, but I still didn't know the whole situation. Campbell had a gun, and I was reasonably sure that whoever was behind me had a gun, too.

Vasquez poked me in the ribs again with his rifle barrel. I would have liked to have shoved that rifle down his throat, but a cool temper must prevail if there was any chance at all of getting out of this alive.

Reluctantly, I walked over toward the fire pit next to Monica. Vasquez motioned me to sit down. Once seated, he tied my hands behind my back while Campbell held a gun on me. Once I was tied, he stepped back.

"Now what, Campbell?" I asked.

"I think it would be a good idea if you just sat there and kept your mouth shut, McCord. Juan doesn't like a lot of talk. It makes him nervous."

After glancing up at Vasquez, I looked at Monica in an effort to find out if she was okay. Other than looking very scared, she seemed to be all right.

"You're a smart man, Campbell. You ought to know that you will never get away with this. You can't just go around killing people. Sooner or later, you will get caught. Besides there are others who know where we are."

"I sincerely doubt that, Mister McCord," a voice behind me said.

This time I turned to see who had spoken. Much to my surprise it was Professor Paul Garvey. I recognized him from the photo on the wall in Sam Kishler's office.

"Well, I must admit that I'm a little surprised to see you here," I said.

"Why? Are you another one of those who think I'm not good enough to find something as important as this?"

"No, not at all. It's just that I thought you were a friend of Sam's."

"Sam was good at what he did, but he wanted to share his find with the rest of the world," he said as if what Sam wanted was a weakness in him.

"What find?"

"This," he said as he waved his arms around to indicate The Great Room.

"And just what is this?"

"It is The Great Room, the meeting place for an entire tribe of ancient Indians who lived here over four hundred years ago, maybe as long ago as when the Spanish expeditions reached into this area. One of the rooms off this one contains all the treasure of those ancient Indians."

"Where? Where is this great treasure? I don't see any treasure, other than the fact that this is an interesting and possibly an important historical find."

He looked at me as if I had slapped him across the face. At first I didn't understand his reaction, but then it came to me. He had no more idea of where the great treasure of the ancient Indians was located than I did. I got the impression that he wasn't even sure that there was any treasure.

It was clear to me that they had been looking around this room, but I doubted that they had had time to look into the rooms at the ends of the tunnels that branched off the main room. It was also clear by the look on his face that they had found nothing of any importance or of any value so far.

He stuttered and looked around as if searching his mind for an answer, but he had none. When he turned back and looked at me, I could see the anger in his eyes. I had obviously struck a tender nerve.

"Forget about him," Campbell said angrily. "He doesn't know anything."

"You shut up, you sniveling little weasel," Garvey yelled back. "He knows more than you think. He probably knows more about what we are looking for than we do."

This sudden exchange of words gave me the impression that Campbell might not be in charge after all, but that Garvey was. It was my first indication that Garvey didn't appear to be the mild, somewhat restrained professor who always stood in Sam's shadow as I had been led to believe. He was assertive and forceful, and Campbell seemed to cower when Garvey spoke sharply. That made it clear that Campbell was afraid of Garvey.

I noticed out of the corner of my eye that Vasquez stood silently off to the side. I got the feeling that he was just waiting for something to happen. I knew from what Roger had told me that Vasquez was not to be trusted. If he was as ruthless a man as his record had indicated, my guess was that he was just waiting for Campbell and Garvey to get into a fight. If that happened, he would kill the one standing and take all the treasure for himself.

If I was right, the only thing keeping him from killing everyone right now was that they had not found the treasure, yet. Once it was found, I was convinced that Vasquez would try to take it all for himself.

Campbell and Garvey walked over to the entrance to one of the tunnels and stood talking for a minute. I could not hear them, but it was clear that Garvey was mad as hell with Campbell. It was clear to me that greed was beginning to show its ugly face. Here were two well-educated men, and one ruthless killer, ready to fight over an unknown treasure like dogs over an old bone.

"Keep an eye on those two," Campbell said to Vasquez.

As I watched them examine one of the hieroglyphics next to one of the tunnels, I noticed that Garvey was doing most of the talking. Campbell did not seem to be as assertive as when I first came into the room. The change in Campbell's manner reinforced my belief that he was not the leader of this expedition.

For the next hour or more, I sat next to Monica. She could not speak to me with a gag over her mouth, but she could help me keep track of Vasquez by looking at him when he was behind me.

While we waited and watched, I worked at getting my hands free. When Campbell and Garvey came out of the first room, they had only a single small stone figure. It was clear that they had not found what they were looking for.

After leaving the figure next to the fire pit, they went on to the next tunnel and studied the hieroglyphics at the entrance. After some discussion that I could not hear, they went into the tunnel.

When they returned to the main room, they had with them some small artifacts that I'm sure had some historic value, but nothing that could be considered a real treasure. I doubted that what they had found so far was worth very much, certainly not enough to kill for. They had obviously expected to find much more, and still might before they finished with the rest of the rooms.

The next room produced nothing more then what they had found in the first two rooms. They had only a small artifact that had little monetary value.

When they got to the fourth small hieroglyphic on the wall, they stopped and stared at the wall next to it. I watched them as they carefully examined the wall. They turned and looked around the room as if they were trying to figure out something.

Suddenly, I realized that they were having the same problem I had with that hieroglyphic. If this part of the wall had been like the rest of the wall, there should have been a tunnel right next to that hieroglyphic, but there was no tunnel.

"It should be here," I heard Garvey say in frustration.

"Well, damn it, it isn't," Campbell replied angrily.

"It has to be. I know it has to be."

"Are you sure you're reading that drawing right?"

"It's a hieroglyph, you imbecile," Garvey retorted. "If you knew anything at all you should know that."

Even from where I was sitting, I could see that Garvey's comment had angered Campbell. Campbell didn't say anything, but I could see him clench his fist as if he would like to reach out and strike Garvey.

Campbell looked over toward us. The expression on his face seemed to suddenly change as he looked at Monica. I saw him reach out and touch Garvey's sleeve. Garvey turned and looked at Campbell, then toward us.

Garvey turned to Campbell. They began to whisper between themselves. I could not hear what they were saying, but I had a feeling that Monica was the topic of their decision.

"Bring her over here," Garvey ordered.

"Don't try to be a hero. Just do as they ask," I whispered as Vasquez untied her feet then moved around behind her.

It angered me when Vasquez grabbed Monica by the arm and lifted her to her feet. I did not like him touching her.

Vasquez pushed her toward Garvey, then stood back and watched. Every once in a while he would glance back over his shoulder at me. The ropes on my wrists were tight and cutting off the circulation to my fingers.

As I watched Garvey pull Monica's gag off, I continued to work on my ropes. If I could get free, we might stand a chance of getting out of here alive. Otherwise, our chances were slim to none. I was sure that they had no intention of letting us live. We knew too much, and they could not allow us to escape from here with what we knew.

"Tell me what this says," Garvey demanded as he pointed at the hieroglyphic.

"You're so damn smart, you figure it out yourself," Monica retorted defiantly.

Without any warning, Garvey slapped Monica across the face, almost knocking her down. I quickly stood, but was met with a rifle barrel firmly jabbed into my stomach. I collapsed on the floor with the wind knocked out of me.

I rolled over and looked back toward Monica as I gasped for air. Garvey had her by the arm and was pointing at the hieroglyphic.

"Tell me what this says," he demanded.

"You're pretty brave slapping a woman when her hands are tied behind her back," I said angrily.

"We don't need him. Vasquez, kill him," Campbell order.

Vasquez looked at Garvey as if he didn't take orders from Campbell. When Garvey nodded, he turned around and pointed his rifle at me.

"No! You kill him and you'll never find the treasure," Monica declared.

"Wait. You tell us what this hieroglyphic says and I'll let him live a little longer. But, if you stall for just one minute, I'll kill him myself," Garvey threatened.

Monica looked at me, then at Garvey. It was clear to me that she had never seen this side of Professor Garvey before.

"Okay," she reluctantly agreed.

Monica began to study the hieroglyph. While she was studying it, I continued to work on my ropes. Vasquez seemed to be as interested in what was going on over by the wall as the rest of them. He only glanced at me occasionally to make sure I hadn't moved.

"Well?" Garvey said, as he grew impatient.

"It.....it indicates....that there should be a tunnel here that leads to a room," she said.

"Where?" Campbell demanded as he, too, was growing impatient.

"Right here," Monica said as she nodded her head toward the wall just to the right of hieroglyphic.

"There's no room or tunnel there," Garvey replied angrily. "It's a solid rock wall."

"And just what's supposed to be in this invisible room at the end of this invisible tunnel?" Campbell asked sarcastically.

Monica hesitated to answer him. I was sure that she knew very well what the hieroglyphic said.

"Well," Garvey yelled.

I saw Monica flinch. It was clear that she was scared, but she had every reason to be.

"It says that the room contains the treasure from the Seven Cities of Cibola."

"You're telling us that the Seven Cities of Cibola had actually existed?"

"No. I'm telling you what the hieroglyph says. The room at the end of the tunnel contains the treasure from the Seven Cities of Cibola," Monica insisted.

If Monica was right, there could be a royal fortune in gold and silver behind that wall. This had to be what Sam was looking for when he was murdered.

I watched as Campbell and Garvey closely examined the wall. I wasn't sure what they would find, but I was sure that once they found what they were looking for, and had no further use for Monica, they would kill both of us.

Campbell pulled his rock pick from his belt, raised his hand up and drove the rock pick down hard against the wall. A large piece of rock fell away from the wall and crumbled to the floor.

"Look," Campbell said with excitement.

"What is it?" Garvey asked.

"It looks like this wall has been plastered with mud made from the rock."

"You mean they sealed up the tunnel?"

"Maybe," Campbell replied as he took his rock pick and began scraping it on the wall.

Large pieces of the wall began falling away as Campbell chipped on the wall. As the rock covering was stripped away, a wall of stone appeared. The tunnel had been sealed up with rock, then covered with a cement-like covering that matched the surrounding wall. It was clear to me that they had found the entrance to the tunnel. If that was the case, we had little time left.

Garvey pushed Monica aside and began helping Campbell chip away at the wall. Monica slowly backed away, moving closer to me. Vasquez grabbed her by the arm and guided her over to the fire pit, sitting her down beside me.

It was easy to see that Vasquez was more interested in what Campbell and Garvey were doing, than in keeping a close eye on us. I continued to work on my ropes. Finally, I was able to work my hands free. I wanted to slip my gun out from under my pant leg, but the lack of circulation in my hands had made my fingers numb. If I grabbed my gun now, I might not be able to hold onto it. I had to have a few minutes to regain the circulation.

"There is a tunnel," Garvey exclaimed.

I could hear the excitement in his voice. We watched as Campbell and Garvey worked feverishly to open the entrance so it was large enough to allow them access to the tunnel.

It took them awhile to get the rocks cleared away enough to allow them to enter the tunnel. Once it was open, Garvey held a lantern up as he looked inside the tunnel.

"Well?" Campbell demanded.

"I can't see much, but it looks like it goes back in there a ways."

"Let's go inside?" Campbell insisted.

"You first," Garvey said.

Campbell hesitated as he looked at Garvey. I got the feeling that Campbell didn't trust Garvey. To my way of thinking, he had every right to be suspicious.

It must have been the thought of riches that compelled Campbell to go ahead and enter the tunnel first. He took his lantern, bent down and entered the tunnel. Garvey quickly followed him.

I watched Vasquez as he walked toward the tunnel. He glanced over at us before he bent down and looked inside.

While he was looking in the tunnel, I reached behind Monica and untied her. She kept her hands behind her as she rubbed her wrists to get her circulation going again.

"Be ready to run," I whispered.

I watched Vasquez as I reached down to my ankle. Just as I was about to pull up my pant leg, I noticed him move. I quickly sat up and put my hands behind my back as if I was still tied. He looked at me for a moment. I was sure he hadn't seen me move, but he stared at me as if he knew something was going on.

Suddenly, there was the sound of loud voices coming from inside the tunnel. It was hard to make out what was being said, but from the sounds of it, Campbell and Garvey had found what they were looking for. There were loud cheers of joy and excitement. I thought I heard something to the effect of "We found it! We found it!"

Vasquez's attention was quickly drawn back to the entrance of the tunnel. He turned his back on us and bent down to look into the tunnel. When he did, I pulled my pant leg up and quickly drew the gun from my boot. Watching him, I motioned for Monica to get down in the fire pit. It was lower than the floor of The Great Room and had a two-foot high wall around the outside. It would provide us with a little protection if I didn't get Vasquez quickly.

Monica dropped down into the fire pit just as Vasquez turned around to check on us. As he raised his rifle, I fired one shot from the 25. caliber automatic, then dove into the fire pit.

It must have been a surprise to Vasquez that I had a gun because he didn't even fire. Instead, he dove into the tunnel to take cover behind the rocks that had been knocked out of the entrance.

Monica and I huddled low in the fire pit as Vasquez took a shot at us. Vasquez's rifle going off filled The Great Room with a deafening noise. Little pieces of rock showered down on us from where the bullet hit the edge of the fire pit.

I took another quick shot over the edge of the fire pit toward the tunnel. I hoped that it would push Vasquez back away from the tunnel entrance, deeper into the tunnel. I saw him move back, then stand up. He was trying to find a better position to shoot from.

Another deafening shot was fired from Vasquez's rifle, but it went wild. The sound seemed to shake the whole place and made my ears ring. I felt a few small pieces of rock fall from the ceiling. I looked up, then at Monica. She was looking at me. From the look in her eyes, I got the feeling that we were both thinking of the same thing. If Vasquez fired that rifle too many times, this whole place could collapse into a pile of rubble.

"I wouldn't shoot that rifle off too many times unless you want to bring this whole place down around your ears," I called out.

"This place has been here for hundreds of years. A little noise isn't going to hurt it any," Vasquez yelled back with a little laughter in his voice.

"Hold your fire, Vasquez," Campbell called out.

"Shut up," Vasquez yelled back.

Just as I looked up over the rim of the fire pit, I saw Vasquez swing his rifle around and point it down the tunnel. I could see Campbell. He was only a few feet from Vasquez.

He was holding a lantern in one hand and something that looked like it might be a gold plate or shield of some kind in the other. I then saw the rifle recoil in Vasquez's hands, and the flash of the muzzle. Campbell fell backward, the lantern and gold plate went flying from his hands. The sound of gunfire once again filled the room.

"He shot Campbell," I said.

I heard another voice from inside the tunnel, then saw Vasquez fire the gun again. This time, the sounds of the rifle echoed through the tunnels and the ground began to shake.

There was no time to waste. I grabbed Monica by the arm and pulled her to her feet. We jumped out of the fire pit and began running across The Great Room toward the tunnel that led to the outside.

"Run," I yelled at Monica.

I heard another shot from behind us and pieces of rock flew off the wall where the bullet struck the wall. I swung around and fired a couple of shots back toward Vasquez in an effort to slow him down, or at least ruin his aim. I then turned back around and ran as fast as I could.

As I started to pass Monica, I grabbed her hand and pulled her along with me. All I could hear from behind us was the sounds of rocks crashing down. I could feel the ground under my feet tremble. There was no need to look back.

Monica stumbled. I quickly pulled her to her feet. I noticed a big cloud of dust was rapidly advancing on us as it rolled through the tunnel. I didn't hesitate. I grabbed Monica by the hand again and started running toward the entrance to the cave as fast as I could.

I could see the light at the end of the tunnel as we ran. The cloud of dust and the deafening sounds of the cave collapsing were gaining on us. When we reached the entrance to the tunnel, we ran out into the sunlight.

# CHAPTER EIGHTEEN

Only a few yards from the entrance to the cave, we fell to the ground and covered our heads. I could not have run any further if I wanted to. I was exhausted.

As the cloud of dust rolled out of the cave entrance, I looked over at Monica. She was breathing hard.

"You all right?" I asked as I gasped for air.

"Yes," she replied breathlessly.

We laid on the cool grass breathing hard. We had managed to escape, but there was no doubt in my mind that the others had been buried in the cave.

I don't know how long we laid in the grass in front of the cave while we tried to catch our breath. I rolled over and sat up. I looked back at the entrance to the cave. It looked the same as it had when we first arrived.

Monica rolled over and sat up, too. I don't know what she was thinking, but I was just happy to be alive.

"You all right?" I asked as I looked back over my shoulder at her.

"I think so."

I stood up and reached down for her hand. She took my hand and I helped her to her feet. I slipped my arm around behind her as we looked toward the cave entrance.

"Do you think any of them might be alive in there?" she asked.

"I certainly doubt it. If they are, they will die in there with the treasure."

I let go of Monica's hand and walked toward the entrance of the cave. I could not see very far inside, and I had no desire to go inside to see how much of the cave had fallen in. I looked down at the ground and saw that the dust and dirt had settled around the entrance of the cave wiping out all traces of anyone ever having been in the cave. Somehow that seemed appropriate to me.

The treasure had been hidden in the cave for hundreds of years. As far as I was concerned, it could remain hidden for hundreds of more years to come.

"What are you doing?" Monica asked.

"Nothing," I said as I turned around and walked back to her.

"What do we do now?"

I looked around. From the position of the sun it was late afternoon. It was going to be dark before long. We had been in the cave for most of the day.

"First of all, I think we should get a good night's sleep. Tomorrow we'll head back."

"What do you think we should do about, you know, Campbell and Garvey?"

"What do you want to do?" I asked.

I watched her as she looked toward the cave and thought about it.

"Nothing," she replied finally.

"Then that's what we will do."

I took her hand and we walked over to the spring. We washed our faces, then walked over to the wall and sat down. We spent some time sitting together on the wall and looking out over the plateau. I wrapped my arm around her shoulder as she leaned against me. We spent this quiet time to watch the sun slowly set in the west.

"Nick, what are we going to tell the authorities?"

"About what?"

"About what happened here."

"Nothing. We never saw Professor Campbell or Professor Garvey. We never found the treasure that Sam was looking for, and never found out who killed him," I said with a matter of fact tone in my voice.

"What are we going to tell Russell Martin about his brother?"

"I think we can tell him that Morris killed his brother. We'll have to talk to the authorities about Morris and Martinez, and how Morris killed Martinez and tried to kill us. The six bullets you put in Morris's chest will have to be explained."

"What will happen to us?"

"I think once we explain to Lieutenant Thompson what happened at the cave where Martin died, he will be able to figure out the rest. We'll just have to tell him that we never found what Sam was looking for or where he was killed."

"In a way that's true. We really never did, at least not for sure," she said.

"I also think that we should destroy the picture map and anything else that might help someone find this place. I think it should remain part of the legend of the Superstition Mountains, forever."

"You're probably right," Monica agreed.

"What do you say we get something to eat, then get some rest? We have a long trip back."

"I have just one more thing to ask. Can we spend a night at the pool again on our way back?" Monica asked with a gleam in her eye.

"I look forward to it. I could use a bath, too," I said as I gently squeezed her against me.

As we walked back to where we had left our sleeping bags, I could not help but think about this beautiful woman beside me. She was the most important person in my life. I had this desire to keep her with me, forever.

"Monica, will you marry me?" I asked as we stopped near our sleeping bags.

Monica turned and looked up at me. A smile came over her face. She threw her arms around my neck and kissed me hard on the lips.

As she pulled back a little, she looked up at me and whispered, "Yes."

We laid down for a while and just rested before we got up and fixed our dinner. After dinner we sat on the wall holding each other and looking out over the grassy plateau. I had to smile and think that all was peaceful once again when I saw the lone coyote bounding off across the plateau.

"I guess our coyote thinks everything is back to normal," I said.

As soon as the sun set, we settled in for some sleep. We were both very tired and needed the rest.

* * *

When morning came, I found myself lying on my back with Monica curled up beside me. It was still dark but the sky was starting to show some light off in the east.

It was a good time to think. The one thing I was thinking about was the trail back. If we took the same trail back that we had used to get here, I had some concerns as to how we were going to get out of the canyon. The walls of the canyon had been very steep. I doubted that the horses could get back up the canyon wall. I had to wonder if there was some other way up here from below.

"What are you thinking about?" Monica said in a whisper.

"I was thinking that it might be a good idea to ride around the rim of the plateau to see if there is another way down from here. Otherwise we might have some difficulty getting out of the canyon."

"It sounds like a good idea."

We laid there for a little while longer before we got up and fixed our breakfast. Monica cleaned up and put out the fire while I gathered the horses and packed our gear on them.

Once we were ready, we mounted up and road over to where we had come up to the plateau from the bottom of the canyon. We then turned and walked the horses along the edge of the plateau. We kept a close eye out for any trail that might take us down without going into the canyon we had used to get up here.

It wasn't long and we found a narrow trail that wondered on down to the desert floor. As we started down the trail, I noticed what looked like tracks left by sheep or goats on the trail. It made it clear how the animals had gotten up to the top of the plateau to enjoy the lush green grass. We decided to take the trail.

About two-thirds of the way down, the trail split. One trail went on around the base of the plateau while the other turned and headed in the general direction of the trail we had taken before we dropped down into the canyon. We took the one toward the trail that we had used before. It wasn't long before we came across the trail that would take us back the way we had come.

It was almost night fall when we got to the place where we had enjoyed the pool formed by the spring. The horses that we had left were still there.

It felt good to have a bath in the cool water and too spend some time just relaxing. We took the opportunity to relax together in the pool before we went to sleep under the stars.

The next morning we gathered up all the horses and headed off toward the camp sight that had been our jumping off point. When we arrived at the jumping off point, we unpacked the horses and stacked the gear under the trees, then let the horses go free. There was little chance that they would wonder off before we could have someone return and pick them up. There was plenty for them to eat and plenty of good clean water.

We took the jeep that had been left there and drove back to Phoenix. We spent a couple of days with Roger and Maggie. While we were there, we gave our statements to the State Police.

When we returned to Madison, we called Russell Martin and told him about his brother and that the guy who had murdered him had been killed trying to kill us. Martin seemed please with the information. He said that he would send us a check as soon as he received our bill. That was good news to us.

Now it was time for Monica and me to take a little time to relax and think about our future together.

Made in the USA
Columbia, SC
14 July 2021

41836116R00134